# *Magical Blend*

## A PARAMOUR BAY MYSTERY
### BOOK ONE

## KENNEDY LAYNE

# DEDICATION

Jeffrey—We finally wrote our cozy mystery series with witches! Thank you for taking this journey with me!

Cole—By now, you've started your first year of college and are unraveling your own mysteries! We love you!

*USA Today Bestselling Author Kennedy Layne switches creative gears and brings you a cozy paranormal mystery that will have you wishing these unique and comical characters could spring to life with a twitch of your nose...*

An inherited tea shop, a quaint little Connecticut town, and its quirky residents have Raven Marigold believing her luck is about to change for the better. Of course, that was before she and her best friend found a dead body in the back of the charming store. Things go from bad to worse when Raven begins to hear a talking cat spouting on and on about magic and mayhem.

Once Raven accepts that she's not losing her mind, she finds herself in the middle of a murder investigation while discovering her family's unusual lineage—the Marigolds are bona fide witches!

Tis the season to be scared and delighted...this wickedly charming tale includes magical tea blends, an enchanting spell book, and an eerie cottage on the edge of town that contains a special surprise you won't want to miss!

# Chapter One

"ARE THEY STILL staring?"

I wasn't sure why I asked that question, considering my back was burning like my favorite linen blouse had been set on fire. I was almost certain I saw some ash floating away on the currents of the mild shore breeze, but the stress I was under had my thoughts a bit muddled.

There was nothing worse than being the center of attention in a village this small. I couldn't imagine drawing more attention than had I been dancing in the streets without a lick of clothing.

Unfortunately, my unannounced presence in the tiny town of Paramour Bay certainly had tongues wagging like the latest E. L. James novel.

Maybe this was a bad idea, after all.

I should have stayed in New York and let the lawyer figure out a way to get me out of this bind.

"Wouldn't you be staring if you were them?" Heidi wiggled her fingers at the townsfolk who were apparently still standing and gossiping on the opposite side of the street. She even flashed them a wide smile through the large display window once we were inside the small store, never one to hide from the limelight. "You're the wicked witch's granddaughter, according to the executor of her will."

"I really don't think Larry Butterball meant to use the word witch."

Having only one memory of my grandmother, her estate lawyer might very well be correct in his assumption. Rosemary Marigold had been a woman who wouldn't waste her time to kick a person where the sun didn't shine. She just took down names and kept walking.

Unfortunately, it was her daily walk that did her in.

A heart attack right there at the intersection of River Bay and Brook Cove.

I know what you're thinking. I should be grieving over the death of my Nan. Wouldn't any decent granddaughter be sad that her grandmother had passed on to the other side? The thing of it was, I hadn't really known her at all. She'd cut me and my mother out of her life a long time ago.

Which made the news of my inheritance all that much more confusing.

I found it very hard to believe that Nan would own something as gentle and restful as a tea shop. Don't get me wrong, I'm sure she was a kind soul to those folks who knew her. And tea would have absolutely benefited her disposition from what I could remember of her, but something just didn't sit right with me about this place.

The tea shop was nothing like the cafés in the city where you placed an order, a barista made the perfect cup of sanity, and you were served over a counter like children at the local school cafeteria. There was actually something quite relaxing about being part of a society where people continued to do the same thing the same way, day after day.

I couldn't imagine Paramour Bay being like that, though.

No, the people here were oddly different. And this quaint little shop was something out of a Hallmark movie, right down to the small gold tassels hanging from the outside awning. The plate glass window even looked to be a century old, with its wavy appearance and bubbled imperfections.

The town could have easily passed as Mayberry from the television show, with the exception of the roads. Those were throwbacks from seventeenth century France. Every intersection between the normally paved streets in Paramour Bay were made of cobblestone, every road was named after some body of water, and the storefronts could have been pulled off the canvas of a Norman Rockwell painting.

The quaint town even had an old pharmacy with ice cream and soda fountain drinks served at the counter by a fresh-faced boy in a white paper hat. I should know, seeing as I peered through the display window next store. I wonder if they still sold penny candy.

Honestly, it was downright eerie. Time seemed to have passed this place by.

Yeah, I should have stayed in the city.

I did a quick sweep of the store. There were shelves upon shelves lined with porcelain teacups, glass jars of various tea leaves, and delicate keepsake trinkets that made me wonder how they'd all survived my grandmother's infamous wrath.

She hadn't been the most maternal woman on the face of the planet. As I said, my mother and I hadn't heard from her in over ten years.

Bottom line?

The entire place was mine, because I was the youngest heir. Nan had apparently wanted to skip everyone else who might have had a claim. And let's face it, my grandmother and mother hated one another more than two old wet hens. I had no doubt that my Nan would have burned this place down to the ground before allowing my mother to step across the threshold. I'm sure there was a lot more grist for the mill, but my mother hadn't been very forthcoming with the rest of the story.

But what was I going to do with a tea shop in the middle of the Connecticut coastline?

"Heidi, I don't know if I can do this."

I chose to stay in the middle of the store, not wanting to be anywhere near the numerous shelves attached to the walls. I tended to be a bit accident prone from time to time. More like a bull in a china shop when I was nervous. It was something I'd come to accept about myself, and I'd rather not be the one who had to clean up all the broken glass. I'd only end up in the hospital getting stitches, giving the old biddies across the street something else to talk about other than the fact that Rosemary's granddaughter had driven into town in a beat-up old Corolla that squealed every time I turned the wheel.

In case you haven't guessed it by now, I don't live the most glamorous of lifestyles.

All of this did raise the question of how I was supposed to get the thin layer of dust off hundreds of potential disasters masquerading as display items. I could hire someone to do it, but that would require money I didn't have. Larry Butterball claimed this place actually made a tidy profit, but I found that hard to believe. We had an appointment this afternoon to go over the financials. I had a feeling that he'd be asking for a check at the end of it all.

Which only went to prove that I had no idea what I was doing with my life.

Financials? I've never had to balance my checkbook, because I've never had enough money left at the end of the month to put in the bank. Well, that was unless a few pennies counted.

Wait.

Did I not tell you my name?

Well, let me introduce myself properly.

I'm Raven Lattice Marigold, reluctant descendant of Rosemary Lattice Marigold. I'm technically the spitting image of her when she'd been younger, only much nicer to children and old folks.

Sometimes.

When I remember my manners.

There was a time or two I would have made her proud, but those were the very moments that I had disappointed my mother with my short-fused temper.

Oh, and my mother has absolutely no idea I'm here in Paramour Bay.

She's back in New York City, thinking that I went on a run of the mill road trip with Heidi. If she had found out that we were driving to Paramour Bay, I would have had two funerals to attend this week. I only have one decent black dress that was appropriate for such occasions, so that wouldn't have worked out so good for either of us.

"I hate to be the bearer of bad news, but it's not as if you have a choice to make this place work." And this is why Heidi would never have children. She didn't understand the definition of comfort. "You lost your job, you're late on your rent by two months, and you barely had enough money to drive that death contraption you call a car from New York City to Paramour Bay. Face it, Raven. This is it. The end of the road. Your new home. It's your silver lining without the parachute."

I looked around the small shop I'd inherited not even a week ago, still questioning if I was doing the right thing. I was a city girl, through and through. I loved the hustle and bustle of the

Big Apple, the nightlife, and the fact that there was a coffee stand on every single corner of my neighborhood.

Did I mention that I love coffee?

I might actually need the stuff to live.

There was nothing better than that first sip of the day when that zap of caffeine traveled at lightning speed to every nook and cranny of my exhausted brain. Honestly, it was pure heaven with all circuits firing.

So why did I think taking over my grandmother's tea shop was a better idea than looking for a new job? I knew nothing about tea, leaves, or...

"What does *eves* even mean?"

I'd made a full circle in the middle of the store, still trying to convince myself that I'd made the right choice to leave my entire life back in the city. Behind Heidi was the large odd display window with the name *Tea, Leaves, & Eves* hand-painted in gold script letters to match the ornate tassels. It made me question if Rosemary had actually been my biological grandmother, considering both me and my mother survived on coffee. The only time we ever drank tea was when we were sick.

Oh, and there's something else I didn't mention. My mother's name is Regina. Yes, all the women's names in my family begin with the letter R. And no, I never got an explanation from my mom as to why that was true.

Come to think of it, Regina Marigold hadn't been very forthcoming about anything to do with our family history on her side. She'd cut ties with them back when I was a teenager. The only reason I have memories of my Nan was because she'd come to New York City every couple of years to try and drag my mother back to her childhood hometown. Those volatile visits suddenly stopped around the time I turned eighteen. Neither one of us addressed that particular falling out, even after we received word of my Nan's death.

I began to realize how self-centered I was to ignore my lineage. The shame was quite stifling in retrospect, but I turned it into motivation that maybe this silver lining as Heidi had dubbed it was exactly what I needed—a sort of homecoming.

"Maybe your grandmother couldn't come up with anything else to rhyme with tea or leaves," Heidi said about the name of the shop, shrugging off what was sure to bother me until I figured out that miniscule mystery. "Didn't Mr. Butterbaum say that your grandmother left some boxes for you to look through? Do you think they're here or at her house? They might be in the back room."

"Butterball," I automatically corrected, as I'd been doing for the last three days. I glanced past the painted sign to see how many of the town's residents were still gawking at the newcomer. Technically, my mother was born here. Didn't that make me a local of sorts? "At least the crowd is finally dispersing."

"Oh, I'm sure they'll be back the minute you flip over the open sign. Did you notice the way that lady with the purple hair put her hand over her heart at the first sight of you? It was as if your Nan had come back from the dead." Heidi walked through the shop, and I had to bite my lip to scream at her not to touch anything. She wasn't exactly known for her graceful movements, either. In New York, everyone bumped into everyone. It was expected. It was just the way the city worked, and no one blinked an eye at the rapid pace we called life. "You know, I can always switch to tea from coffee if you give me a ten percent discount. I'd be willing to try it out, at least."

Heidi lifted up what looked like an upside-down whisk, though I had no idea what it could be used for. Didn't one just dip a tea bag in water and voila? A cup of tea didn't require an advanced degree in chemistry, did it?

It was rather fun to see Heidi raise her perfectly waxed, manicured eyebrow a half inch.

"Better make that twenty percent. Oh, and free shipping." Heidi shook her head as she set down the contraption. "No wonder Butterbaum said this place gets a fairly decent profit."

I didn't bother to correct Heidi this time on Larry Butterball's name. She wasn't going to be here long enough for that to matter, anyway. A nervous flutter began to flurry in my stomach. I wasn't ready to be stranded alone in a small town all by myself with only three hundred and fifty-four complete strangers.

Did I mention that Paramour Bay was all the way up the coast in the middle of Connecticut?

I suppose I should catch you up on my life. So, let's freeze this scene while Heidi checks out the rest of the shop for interesting items that could help me out in the near future.

You see, I was born to Regina Lattice Marigold twenty-nine years ago in New York City. She never told me who my father was, only that my grandmother hadn't approved of her choice of men. Mom and Nan had fought for years about where I should be raised, but somehow, my mother came out the victor. I guess what they say about possession being nine tenths of the law was right. And let me clarify this right now, that was probably the only battle she'd ever truly won over Rosemary.

The women in my family tended to be headstrong. I recall my grandmother once mentioning that we had distant cousins, though I never met any of them personally.

Care to guess why?

Bingo!

Apparently, there was some huge rift between Rosemary and

her sister regarding a man, of all things. The two went their separate ways with bad blood between them, and my Nan ended up here in Paramour Bay to raise her daughter without any family. I'm relatively sure the man my Nan and Aunt Rowena argued over was my grandfather, but no one had ever confirmed that, nor had I ever heard his name.

We all have hair so black that there are times I would swear it shimmers purple, which is not exactly my favorite color. It does, however, suggest that my own heritage might lean toward the southern European side. Green eyes run in our family, as does high cheekbones and full lips that I thank my genetics for every day. Other than that? I must have gotten my hips from the other side of my family whom we shall not mention.

Anyway, after I graduated high school, I made the foolish decision not to go to college right away. I worked as a receptionist for various businesses over the years, having gotten rather good at dealing with disgruntled clients and such. Unfortunately, those types of positions are being replaced by computer generated voices. Envision the afternoon I had to tell my mother that I'd lost my job to a computer.

It hadn't been very pleasant for either one of us.

Oh, and don't think I haven't thought of taking night classes here and there to get my degree. It was actually what I was researching on my phone when a call came through from a number I hadn't recognized.

I don't know what made me answer, but I swiped the screen to the right out of habit. And that was when Larry Butterball entered the picture.

My grandmother, Rosemary Lattice Marigold, had dropped dead of a heart attack on her daily walk. She'd formally requested a small funeral service with only her daughter and granddaughter in attendance.

You can imagine how awkward that day had been, with both of us sitting alongside a gravesite wearing black for a woman we basically hadn't seen in over a decade. On top of that, it was with a man by the name of Larry Butterball. He'd been sweating like he'd just gotten out of the oven. And yes, he absolutely resembled a done-up turkey in his black double-breasted suit, only without the red button sticking out of his belly.

It wasn't until after the service that Mr. Butterball came up to me and discreetly handed me an official-looking envelope. I didn't open it until I'd returned to my one room apartment that was overtop an all-night diner. I'd been surprised when the contents of the envelope contained information regarding a reading of my grandmother's will. It had taken place the following day, but my attendance had been the only one required.

I knew then that my mother had been cut out of the will. It seemed my Nan had gotten in one last jab from the grave. Hence, why I haven't told my mom that I was coming to Paramour Bay. She would have been hurt, rightfully so, and she would have absolutely had me try and sell the place so that I didn't have to set foot in the town in which she'd been born.

Only problem?

My grandmother had made a stipulation in her will that was ironclad—under no circumstances could I sell the tea shop until at least twelve months had passed from the date of her death.

Another itsy-bitsy clause stated yet one more thing that I haven't mentioned. I would have to reside in Paramour Bay for those twelve months or else the proceeds of the sale would go to…get this…a super strange wax museum on the edge of town.

"What the heck is that?"

The horror that laced Heidi's tone had me spinning around to look at the back of the store. I saw nothing that could have garnered that type of response.

"What?"

I darted my eyes over to the small counter in the back corner, where Heidi's attention had been drawn. There was nothing there but a cash register and a feathered pen sticking out of its holder. Was that what Heidi was pointing out? The feathered pen in place of the usual black credit card machine?

"Um, nothing." Heidi was frowning, which was never a good thing. She tilted her head to the side, studying the feathered pen. "I could have sworn…"

Heidi's voice trailed off as she started to weave through the various high-top tables that were positioned for guests to sample specific teas. You realize that this means I have to use my evenings from now until the end of time to research tea leaves, their different flavors, the numerous ways to properly make the so-called civilized beverage, and how to actually make it taste good, right?

I suspect several cubes of sugar would have a great deal to do with that.

I tried to quell my panic, because it wouldn't do me any good. I was stuck here for twelve months, whether I liked it or not. But that didn't mean I had to be here all alone.

"Are you sure you can't get a few more days off? After all, there was a funeral."

I wasn't happy that Heidi had to return to New York City in the morning, but at least she'd been able to accompany me on the long drive here. She worked in accounting at the place where I used to answer phones, but she'd been smart and gotten her degree at night school.

Fortunately for me, she'd been able to take a long weekend to escort me here to this tiny speck on the map. She had stood watch and made sure my mother didn't accidentally see me packing all of my belongings into the back of my beat-up Corolla. She was everything a friend should be, but she would be over a hundred miles away should something go horribly wrong.

I briefly wondered if there was a way to avoid the train Heidi would be catching at some ungodly hour before the sun rose, but I did need her to be back in the city before I called my mother to break the news of my recent relocation to the northern coastline.

"I used up all my vacation time when I went to Maui with Patrick." Heidi fanned herself as she forgot all about whatever bothered her a few moments ago. She'd been head over heels with Patrick ever since he'd removed his shirt to fix a pipe underneath her sink. "And it was totally worth it. Besides, you'll be fine here. It's only for twelve months, right? Then you can come back to the city, where we'll return to our wicked little ways."

I had to laugh at Heidi's description of our personal lives. Wicked was on the totally opposite end of the spectrum from which we existed. We were both closing in on our thirties, and our ever-changing views of the dating world, the work force, and basically our future had snuck up on us when we weren't even looking.

I wasn't sure I was ready for my thirties, but I certainly couldn't stop time from marching on.

"Heidi, you're right." I held up my hand so that she didn't get the wrong idea. It was time for me to stand on my own two feet. "I'm talking about me taking the bull by the horns here. It's only a measly twelve months. I'll do what I can to see that Nan's shop supports me for at least that long, and then I can sell it for enough of a profit that will help me finally take those college courses without having to work two jobs to afford the tuition."

"That's the spirit!" Heidi looked at her watch before tucking her blonde strands of hair behind her ear. "You said we're meeting Butterbaum for lunch at Trixie's Diner, right? We have another thirty minutes before we need to be there. Let's take a look in the back of the shop and see if we can't find out why your grandmother named the shop *Tea, Leaves, and Eves*. You've got to admit, it's kinda cute sounding."

That's the thing.

My Nan hadn't been cute.

She had been a force to be reckoned with, which was why I found it so hard to believe that she loved tea over the rich, inviting taste of coffee.

Rosemary Marigold had long black hair, of course, but even longer nails that had always been polished a dark red. She'd also worn matching lipstick. She'd been beautiful in her own way, always wearing whimsical clothing with sleeves that went past her wrists and skirts that were more colorful than a peacock's feathers on display. But there had always been something peculiar in the way she observed people when she'd walk around the city. It was as if she knew something they didn't.

I still didn't understand fully what caused Nan to never come back to New York. Had the strife between mother and daughter finally been too much to bear?

How could a mother cut off a daughter as if she never existed?

My family was very strange, indeed.

Of course, I might find out the reason why they parted ways after my impending call with my mother. I couldn't do it now, though. I would wait until Heidi was back in the city before delivering my news. That way, she could intervene on my behalf and supply some red wine to soften the blow that her only daughter was giving up twelve months of her life to live in a town she'd wanted nothing to do with for most of her adult life.

"If you ever met my Nan, you'd understand that *cute* wasn't her kind of thing. And those hanging antique ivory-colored beads in place of a door that leads to the back room? Nan had her own rather unique style, and let me tell you that it was quite expensive. It was rare that she owned plastic anything, unless she'd resorted to plastic surgery in her old age."

I carefully walked around one of the high-top tables that held two teacups that appeared to be real bone china, along with a matching teapot. The delicate pink roses on the tableware were stunningly beautiful, and honestly nothing even remotely similar to the taste of décor that my grandmother would have preferred.

Something was really off here, but I couldn't put my finger on it just yet.

Maybe the Nan I remembered had changed and become one of the old biddies across the street with greying hair and matching sweaters. I should look for a recent picture among the piles of belongings. Didn't everyone change a smidgen in their old age? Soften a bit? Maybe the regret of choosing to live all on her own had finally made her see that life hadn't been meant to be so lonely.

The odd whitish cast of beads I was referring to earlier prevented customers from seeing into the storage room. One's gaze automatically focused on the ivory shapes cut into…fairies. I mean, they were actually fairies stacked on top of one another. It was if they were dancing a spectral spiraling pirouette that one couldn't look past. I assumed it was hiding a storage room for stock items. What else would be in the back of a tea shop?

I needed to alter my way of thinking and try to picture the next twelve months as an adventure of sorts. This could benefit me in long run, because surely Nan kept some kind of written records regarding our family history. This could be like a treasure hunt, providing me with the answers my mother would never bother to divulge.

For the first time since leaving New York City, my heart fluttered with a flicker of excitement.

Heidi was the first to slip her fingers in between the magical beads, causing each single hand-carved shape to emanate a never-ending string of melodic clicks as they ricocheted off one another. The soft tactile click made me smile in anticipation of what we would find.

"Um, Raven?"

The thing about being best friends with someone was knowing when he or she was being overly dramatic and when things were really, really wrong.

In this case?

A lump of fear formed in my throat. I expected the worst. You know, an overly large rat with big yellow teeth or maybe a spider's web that had been given a week to create the most horrifying trap that would enable him to cocoon an entire human body.

Did I mention that I have an overactive imagination?

"What's wrong? And don't tell me a wasp's nest is back there, because I don't have my EpiPen with me. It's somewhere in my luggage in the back of the Corolla."

"What about an inhaler?"

"I don't have asthma."

"You're about to."

Heidi stepped aside so that I could look through the strings of diverting fairies.

She was right. I was suddenly having a very hard time breathing.

"Is that…"

"Larry Butterbaum? Yes. Do you think the poor guy had a heart attack or something?"

"Butterball, Heidi. His name was Larry Butterball, like the turkey."

One would think that at some point in my life that my luck would change for the better. I honestly thought it had, but the dead body in my newly acquired tea shop told me the tide hadn't turned just yet.

"Well," Heidi said in what I took as an attempt to make me feel better. Let me just forewarn you that she utterly failed. "Welcome to Paramour Bay."

# Chapter Two

WHO WOULD HAVE thought such a small town had 911?
A sweet woman had answered, who assured me that she would immediately be sending over Sheriff Drake. She offered her own theory that I must be mistaken about Larry Butterball having a heart attack, because the man had been in excellent shape for someone his age. I tried to explain to her that we must be talking about two completely different people, because I couldn't understand how anyone describing the man I knew as Larry Butterball as being healthy by any stretch of the imagination.

This Larry that was currently lying dead in the backroom of my newly acquired tea shop had been carrying quite a bit of extra weight around his waistline.

"I feel as if we should wipe our prints off those ivory-colored beads," Heidi whispered, both of us huddled by the door about as far away from the storeroom as we could possibly get without leaving the shop.

The sun was still shining, no one stood on the other side of the street staring at the front of the shop any longer, and it appeared to be a beautiful day in the month of October. The air had contained a hint of fresh crisp wind early on when we'd driven into town, and I had to admit that not breathing in the everyday pollution of the city was rather refreshing.

It had actually been welcoming, almost as if something inside of me had longed for the peaceful qualities a place like this offered. I had understood that being in the countryside was vastly different, and that it would give the impression of being on vacation for the first week or two until realization set in.

So how had all that promise of a bright new future been blackened by the discovery of a dead body five minutes after arriving at my newly inherited business? Why me? Was this some form of bad karma unloading on me for planning to sell the tea shop in twelve months and running away with a tidy profit?

Heidi's words about wiping our fingerprints off all the hard surfaces brought my attention back around to the issue at hand.

"I thought you said he had a heart attack."

"How would I know? I'm not a medical examiner."

"What if he *was* murdered?"

I don't know why my mind always went straight to the morbid side of things, but then again, I did have a bad habit of reading those cozy mysteries where Aunt Agatha found Uncle Darcy dead in the library. The weapon was usually a candlestick or the rope.

But this wasn't a novel or one of those mystery movies where the lovely misunderstood heroine solved the murder and then went on to live happily ever after.

I had bills to pay and a life to construct.

"At least we have each other as an alibi. That works, right?"

I couldn't believe we were standing here talking about alibis when a man was dead in the other room.

Dead.

"Do you think he was married?" I asked, harboring some serious guilt at the moment, heavier than the suitcase in the trunk of my car. "I never even thought to ask."

If Larry Butterball had a wife or children, they would be devastated. His wife would now be facing a life alone, and I for one understood that it wasn't all it was cracked up to be.

"I didn't see a wedding ring." Heidi eventually pointed through the glass pane of the front door and whistled in the way she did when someone attractive caught her attention. That kind of behavior certainly wasn't acceptable in this situation, so I backhanded her softly across the arm. It didn't help at all. "And I don't see one on him, either."

*Him* turned out to be the man they were waiting on—Sheriff Drake. At least, according to the badge and nametag pinned to his khaki uniform shirt, which seemed to go with the general theme set by his blue jeans and cowboy boots. There was no denying that he was attractive. Rugged good looks had been paired with a healthy amount of sun to accent his features. He was probably five or six years older than me, at least six feet tall with a natural wave in his brown hair, and matching eyes that looked anything but cheerful at the moment.

I couldn't help but match his frown with my own.

No wonder he wasn't married.

Heidi and I stepped back in unison, unable to keep our eyes off Sheriff Drake's intimidating form as he crossed the street. His strides were even and determined as he pursued his duties. The gold little bell chimed overhead as he stepped inside, the atmosphere becoming rather ominous.

"Ms. Marigold?" His eyes immediately connected with mine, telling me that Nan hadn't totally lost her appeal if she'd gone grey and given up her whimsical wardrobe. I told you we looked alike, and my flowing skirt only clinched his observation that I must have been the one who called the station. I liked the gypsy style of clothes as well, but my apparel usually came from lower end stores in the city than the trendy local shops that Nan must have frequented. "I'm Sheriff Liam Drake. What is this about Larry having a heart attack? An ambulance should be here shortly."

"I think it's a little late for that, Sheriff."

"What Heidi is trying to say is that, well, we believe he's dead." I blinked furiously to erase the image of the man's unfocused gaze staring up at the ceiling. I've watched my share of movies, and I have to say that dead bodies look nothing like they do in real life. "He's, um, in the storage room."

Sheriff Drake appeared to want to say something else, but he remained silent as he gracefully walked across the small store and through the fairy beads. Neither Heidi nor I spoke a word as we apprehensively waited for him to come back through the doorway.

We must have remained in place for at least thirty seconds before we allowed ourselves to take a breath.

Then another twenty.

Sheriff Drake still didn't join us back in the main shop.

"The ambulance is here," Heidi said, not needing to verbalize the obvious. The loud siren had caught the attention of several residents walking up and down the sidewalk. A crowd was beginning to form once again. This wasn't how I'd pictured my first introduction to my neighbors of Paramour Bay. "And the purple-haired lady is back, too."

Everyone's attention was now on *Tea, Leaves, and Eves*, even the old biddie who'd watched us enter the shop. And she wasn't alone.

It was something I didn't want or need, so I took matters into my own hands.

"You go ahead and let the paramedics in, and I'll go see

what's taking the sheriff so long."

What was Sheriff Drake doing behind those shimmering beads? I mean, how long did it take to confirm that someone didn't have a pulse?

Unless the death of Larry had been more of a personal issue.

*Oh, my.* Had they been related in some way?

I quickened my steps as I made my way to the back, connecting dots that might very well not even be there. Were they uncle and nephew? Were they cousins? They had different names, so one would assume they'd come from different sides of the families.

Before I could enter the back or come up with any other plausible relationship between the two men, Sheriff Drake's large form materialized through the tiny ivory-colored carvings strung together on cords. I was forced to take a step back.

"I need you to stay out here, ma'am."

*Ma'am?* I was twenty-nine years old. Ma'am was my mother, but I didn't dare to correct him. He was only being courteous, and I didn't want to cause him any more trouble than I already had with my call into 911.

"Is he…"

I don't know why I worded that as a question, when I was positive that Larry Butterball was dead. It had something to do with the color of the man's skin. Or maybe the sightless eyes.

"Yes, he's dead." Sheriff Drake rested a hand on my shoulder, as if he were bracing me for some horrible news. It was a comforting touch, but it nowhere near made up for his following statement. "But the man on the floor back there isn't Larry Butterball."

"Of course, he is. Was. That *was* Larry Butterball. He was the lawyer who handled my grandmother's will."

"Larry does handle most of the estates here in town, but I've never seen the man lying on the floor back there." Sheriff Drake was shaking his head to someone behind me, but I was still reeling from his announcement and didn't bother to turn and see who he was waving off. "And whoever he was, he didn't die from any heart attack. That man was murdered."

"M-murdered?"

This had to be karma biting me in the butt.

Nothing else made sense.

I thought back over the last week. Mr. Butterball had reached out by phone, but then we met in person at the gravesite. He'd handed me his card, the envelope, and then sat with me and my mother as a few words were spoken by a local pastor. We never even entered the town's limits, though. My mother had already taken a step toward the car before the last word of the service had even been uttered.

"Wait." I had concrete proof that the dead man in there was Larry Butterball. "I drove here to meet with Mr. Butterball at his office four days ago. His office is on Lake Drive. I can even show you where we met, if you'd like."

"Ma'am, Larry is—"

"Please call me Raven," I interrupted, having enough of the ma'am stuff. I needed to concentrate, and he was making that almost impossible under the circumstances by constantly telling me I didn't know what I was talking about. My observation was simple enough to prove. "Is your Mr. Butterball's office on Lake Drive?"

"Yes, but—"

"Then that *is* Larry Butterball—my grandmother's lawyer."

"Raven, I grew up with Larry," Sheriff Drake said, all but destroying any hope of having this be a simple misunderstanding. "He's thirty-six years old, six feet three, and bald. The man lying dead on your floor in the back of the shop might be the man you met, but he is definitely not Larry Butterball."

# Chapter Three

"IT WILL BE okay," Heidi assured me with a pat on my arm before she opened the passenger door of my Corolla. I found it difficult to trust that she could truly believe that herself, but the tone of her voice betrayed no doubt. "Your Sheriff Drake will get to the bottom of this. Look at this as an opportunity to learn more about the day-to-day operations of the tea shop. You said yourself you needed to study the different ways to prepare it, what blends go together, and yada, yada, yada. Now you'll have the time to figure it out."

Heidi waved her hand around and around in the air as she closed the car door, not waiting for me to do the same. I contemplated locking the doors and taking a nap. Honestly, I was completely exhausted after today's events.

Sheriff Drake had released us from the scene of the crime, which just happened to be my only means of making a living at the moment. I know, I was quite shocked that neither Heidi or myself hadn't been thrown in jail, but he'd told us to go home and that he would be in touch regarding the investigation.

Why did I feel as though it wasn't going to be quite as easy as he'd made it sound?

I sighed in frustration and popped the trunk to buy myself a few extra seconds. My eyes drifted back to the small cottage that sat on the edge of town. I wrestled with the memory of my grandmother in contrast to the one-story house in front of me. There was absolutely no way that Nan had lived here, but Heidi had checked the address twice.

This was Rosemary Marigold's property, alright. And now it was mine.

Fake Larry Butterball had referenced Rosemary as a wicked witch. I thought he'd been referring to her using a rather base vernacular, but seeing what could pass for the eerie house that Hansel and Gretel stumbled upon in the forest might have had something to do with it. The place was practically overgrown, looking more like a gardener's worst nightmare than an occupied residence.

It didn't help that a wrought iron fence surrounded the small yard, with each post having an ominously sharp spike on the end. The two trees on either side of the yard were beginning to lose their leaves, and I could just imagine what the entire scene in front of me would look like in the dead of winter.

Again, an uneasy tingle began to make its way up my spine. Just maybe the old fake turkey's description hadn't been too far off the mark.

What was going on in this tiny town of Paramour Bay?

Was there another reason my mother left here without ever looking in the rearview mirror beside my grandmother? Had my mom sought to escape the embarrassment of living in a hovel nearly reclaimed by the gnarled hands of the untamed shrubbery?

An abrupt knock on the window practically stopped my heart.

"Are you coming or what? I don't know about you, but I could sure use a glass of wine. Maybe even a shot of whiskey."

Heidi hadn't cared that there was a pane of glass between us.

She'd raised her voice and made her intentions known with a wide smile. It was a good thing that this particular plot of land was around a half mile from town, yet still within the city limits.

How could Heidi smile so pleasantly all the while knowing a man was dead?

I opened my door, having no intention of dragging everything from my vehicle to the house. At least, not all tonight. The completely jam-packed trunk and the sheer number of sundry items in the backseat made the car look like it belonged to some hoarder. Two different style suitcases took up most of the trunk, but piles of clothes that wouldn't fit in the two cases, shoes, boxes, and miscellaneous items were all stacked on top of one another. It was why I'd packed an overnight bag, which I quickly grabbed from the floorboard behind my seat.

"Did you hear what Sheriff Drake said about good ol' Fake Larry?"

"That he wasn't actually the real Larry?"

"No, the part about how there hasn't been a murder in Paramour Bay in over fifty years." I found that bit so hard to believe, but who was I to question the sheriff? He didn't seem too talkative, anyway. "Fifty-three years, to be exact."

I stepped ahead of Heidi and flipped the latch on the gate, wincing when the hinges squeaked as if the pivots had forgotten to be oiled since they had been installed. It looked somewhat new, so I had to wonder if it hadn't been put together properly to begin with. Had Nan been ripped off by the sham door-to-door installers? It happened all the time in New York, but I would think things would be different out here in a small town.

"What does fifty-three years have to do with anything? We weren't even born yet," Heidi pointed out, walking through the gate first. We both strolled down the cobblestone walkway, stopping at least twenty feet before what could only be the front step. I was pretty sure it was a flat slab of rock to match the rest of the house. Either way, it appeared dark gray in the shadows of the setting sun, and reclaimed by the same half-dead tentacles as the rest of the house. "And it wasn't like you killed Fake Larry. Sheriff Drake can take that sexy swagger right out the door if he believes otherwise."

I decided not to mention that fifty-three was my mother's age. There were too many unanswered questions here as it was, and if I mentioned that fact, Heidi might very well decide to drive back to town to remedy that quandary. There was no need to throw anything else into the recipe. The pot was bubbling over already. I had twelve months to find out all of Paramour Bay's dirty little secrets.

I shivered as a cool breeze came off the lake behind the cottage. The temperature had dropped quite precipitately this evening, so it was no wonder the welcoming scent of burning firewood drifted through the air. The bright orange sunset glistened off the still water, but it wouldn't be long before it was dark as the moonless sky.

Fall was suddenly in the air.

"We should either go inside or pitch a tent."

I tried to steer my thoughts to what treasures this house held, considering I wasn't allowed in the back of the tea shop until Sheriff Drake gave the all clear. He'd actually called in the state police, who in turn had grilled me for the past six hours. I told my side of the story three times before they all seemed to believe me, especially given that Heidi had said the exact same things when they'd turned their attention toward her.

"You have the key Fake Larry gave you, right?"

I did, right on the keychain in my hand. Something held me

back from closing the distance to the front door. It was then that the wreath hanging in the middle of the wooden entrance caught my attention.

I'd seen it before.

"Heidi, that's betony."

"Who's Bethany?" Heidi asked, scanning the yard for a person when I meant the purple perennials. "Where?"

"Not who, but what."

"What?"

I shook my head at the confusing conversation. I pointed toward the wreath, finally moving closer to the front step. This was exciting for me. I'd read up on tea leaves on the Internet, choosing the most reputable sites I could find, and discovered the various flavors from different herbs and leaves. And if I remembered correctly, this particular flower was used to cure many ills.

"The wreath is made of betony. It's an herb used to blend with tea." My spirits lifted at the fact that I knew more than I thought I did, so I lifted the key in small victory. "I wonder why she made it into a wreath?"

Heidi was behind me as I slid the key into the slot, but she tapped me in the middle of the back, preventing me from twisting it. And she didn't stop until I finally turned around. All I wanted to do was see the inside of the cottage. Was that too much to ask?

I had numerous questions that needed answering.

Would the interior resemble the outside with its strange haunted vibe? Would there be answers regarding who Fake Larry was and why he'd pretended to be another person altogether? Would this house contain the answers to the questions I had about my lineage?

Heidi was still tapping me, though I'd turned enough that she was now hitting my stomach. I brushed her hand away in irritation while following her gaze. My heart skipped a beat, maybe two, as I caught sight of a large man standing on the other side of the gate. All I could think was that it was a good thing it was closed, because that small blessing would give me and Heidi time to run. If we could make it to the backyard, we could always try and swim to safety.

"Hello."

"Um, hello?" That was the second time today that I worded a statement as a question. The man was still as a statue, and he didn't seem inclined to say anything else or to gain entrance. I prodded him along. "Can we help you?"

"I'm Ted."

"Ted Bundy," Heidi muttered underneath her breath, certainly not talking about the man's looks. He was at least six feet and six inches tall, if not more. He had yellowish blond hair and what appeared to be sunken eyes. I couldn't really tell from where we were standing. "We should run all the way back to the city."

"Stop it," I murmured just as low so that my voice didn't carry in the slight breeze.

We both waited for the strange man to continue, but all he did was remain standing where he was while staring at the two of us with curiosity. Well, it was a two-way street.

Speaking of streets, I tore my gaze away from the mysterious Mister Ted. I scanned the area and couldn't fathom where he'd come from or even from which direction he might have approached us. As I said, this property was located a half mile from town. There were no neighbors and no trails that I could see.

"Hello, Ted."

"You look just like her."

Ted had to be talking about Nan, but I wasn't convinced this guy was on the right side of sanity. For one, he wore a suit. He kind of resembled an undertaker. Wait. Did he work for the funeral home that had buried Nan?

"I do look like her," I replied, not knowing what else to say. Heidi was still pulling at the hem of my shirt, but I kept batting away her hand. "I'm Raven, Rosemary's granddaughter."

Another round of silence lasted at least forty-five seconds. And while that doesn't seem to be long, trust me, it felt like an eternity.

"Ted, do you live somewhere around here?"

"Yes."

"Raven, do you think—"

"I live around back."

Ted hadn't known that he was interrupting Heidi, but his answer certainly had her shutting up.

What did he mean around back? He wasn't talking about some sort of shed in the yard, was he?

Heidi and I slowly stepped off the flat rock in unison and just as gradually made our way to the side of the house. Sure enough, what appeared to be a large shed overlooked the lake. It didn't look nearly large enough to accommodate such a big man.

And no longer was the sun shimmering off the water. The sun had left us to our own devices, leaving us here alone with Ted in the diminishing twilight.

"I'm ready to run," Heidi whispered, clutching her overnight bag. "Are you ready to run? Where are the keys? We could use them as a weapon."

I didn't have the heart to tell her that I'd left the keys in the door. It was better for her not to know and die thinking we stood half a chance of survival.

Hope was a powerful emotion.

"I can put these inside."

Heidi shrieked after we both realized that Ted had somehow come through the gate without a single squeak. How had he done that? I managed to keep both feet rooted on the ground, but I was no longer beginning to think something was strange about Paramour Bay.

I was absolutely positive this place was totally off its rocker.

The knee-high boots I wore underneath my skirt were luckily flat. They would have come in extra handy had I expended any energy to make a run for it, but something peculiar happened that changed my mind.

Ted smiled.

Well, he tried to smile with the collection of broken teeth he had.

He reminded me of a lost boy, eager to find someone to tell him what to do.

He was also standing there with practically everything I'd packed in the backseat of my car. Again, it made me wonder how he'd gotten through the gate without making a sound, but it no longer mattered. He was obviously a friend of my Nan's. Otherwise, why would she allow him to live on the property?

Could Ted be some type of groundskeeper? Maybe I could ask him to take a whack at the shrubbery.

"Thank you, Ted." I rushed over to open the door for him, ignoring the look of incredulity on Heidi's face. It was a good thing I had a bottle of wine tucked away. It would help her come to terms with leaving me here come morning. "That's awfully sweet of you."

Ted made his way into the small cottage before us, followed by me, because Heidi wasn't going anywhere near Ted. I didn't blame her, but something told me that Ted was entirely harmless.

"Oh, wow."

I came up short, allowing Ted to walk farther into the absolutely stunning cottage. It was much larger on the inside than it looked from the outside.

"Oh, wow, indeed," Heidi said a little breathlessly. The view of the interior took her attention off Ted. "You know, I can quit my job to help you. We could split the profits. You do the research while I socialize with the local talent."

I understood her offer. Man, I totally did. And to say I was thanking my lucky stars to have a Nan who had such good taste was an understatement. This was the Nan I remembered. I made a mental note to grill my mother about why the two of them hadn't gotten along. It was time I get some answers.

It wasn't like I could put off calling her for much longer, considering the police would want her statement regarding Fake Larry. She would need to answer some of their questions as well.

"Did you not have a home?"

Ted's odd question in such a sad tone made me realize he took Heidi's reaction in the literal sense.

"We live in apartments in New York City, but we're just surprised by the interior, is all. Nan had great taste. This place is absolutely beautiful."

And it was, with all the surprisingly modern furniture, updated appliances, and granite countertops. There were splashes of color everywhere, from the burgundy pillows to the gold and blue rugs. The living room furniture was made of cream, overstuffed cushions that a person could sink into and never want to leave.

As for the coffee table, it was the one piece of furniture that stood out the most. It had to have been handmade. The intricate wooden designs were nothing like I'd seen before, and my fingers itched to trace the carvings.

"You will sleep there."

Ted pointed to the wooden railing above the kitchen, signifying a loft bedroom. I would have gone straight up the spiral staircase, but I didn't want to appear rude. Ted had been so nice to carry in the things from my backseat. I automatically reached into my oversized purse and pulled out a few ones.

Ted stared at the money in my hand, making no move to take it.

"It's my way of thanking you, Ted."

"It's a good thing Ms. Rosemary brought you here." Ted reached out, and with the coldest of hands, closed his fingers around my own so that the money was clutched in my palm. "I am not a man of the night. But thank you."

I was so shocked by what Ted was referring to that I could only stare at his perfect posture as he bent his head to duck as he walked out the door. He even closed it quietly behind him so softly that I didn't hear the expected click.

How did he do that?

"Did he think you called him a—"

"Who *is* he?" I asked in confusion, looking down at my hand where the coolness from his touch still remained. How could someone be so cold? "He takes things so literally. And he never did say how he'd come to live in the backyard. Heidi, I've got to tell you that this place is far past the point of freaking me out."

I'd gone through a myriad of emotions throughout the day, ranging from skepticism to horror, and then from excitement to unease. The people in Paramour Bay, maybe with the possible exception of Sheriff Drake, were odd. And that included the older woman with the purple hair who looked as if she'd seen a ghost after she'd set eyes on me. Not even the younger man standing behind her had been able to flush some color in her cheeks.

As for Fake Larry Butterball—who was he, why had he pretended to be someone else, and what had he wanted with me in the first place?

More importantly, why had someone killed him in my tea shop?

"What's wrong with a little mystery when you get to live here?" Heidi dropped her overnight bag on the floor and continued to stare in awe at the beautiful décor. "Let's face it, this place would go for a fortune in the city. The outside needs some work, obviously, but this place is fantastic."

"Well, I remember Nan having great taste in clothes and jewelry. It doesn't surprise me that she would decorate like this, though she was in her late seventies. I would think that this combination of modern and traditional designs wouldn't have been her style at her age."

I took my time spinning on the non-existent heel of my boots, taking in every nook and cranny of this place, not expecting Heidi to cry out in alarm. I instantly hunched my back and covered my head, certain that something horrid was going to attack me.

"There!" Heidi exclaimed, the rapid shuffle of her shoes bringing her ever closer. "Tell me you saw that, Raven. Did you?"

"See what?" I'd had about enough of her setting my nerves on edge when they'd already taken a flying leap into the abyss. I began to think that bottle of wine might steady my nerves, as well. I lowered my hands and was amazed to find Heidi on her hands and knees on the opposite side of the room, looking under a grand hutch that held beautiful wooden bowls, cast iron basins, and numerous items that I'd only ever seen in old television shows. "Heidi, what are you doing?"

"This is the second time I've spotted something…well, orange or black. And maybe furry, I don't know."

Fear kept my boots glued to the hardwood floor. I'd already mentioned that I was terrified of rats. Well, that included mice. I'm pretty sure it had to do something with their beady little red eyes.

"Do you think Paramour Bay is overrun with mice?" I managed to step to the side, trying to see around Heidi to the small space underneath the massive hutch. I saw nothing but the matching baseboard to the hardwood floor, with the exception of a dust bunny or two. "Are you sure that's what you saw?"

Heidi leaned back on her calves, looking around the house in confusion.

"I don't know. It was way too big to be a mouse. Maybe a possum? But they aren't orange. Or black. Or that furry." Heidi shook her head in defeat. "Do you have that bottle of wine?"

A bottle of wine sounded perfect to cap off this strange day. I'd even pushed aside wanting to find those boxes that Fake Larry had mentioned my Nan wanting me to look through. Those could wait until tomorrow.

Right now?

I needed some downtime with my best friend, totally ignoring the possibility that there was a possum in the vicinity that had disappeared into thin air.

Come tomorrow, I would be on my own with a murder

investigation looming over me, a sheriff who didn't know me, a strange giant living in my back yard, and a bizarre house that was incredible on the inside yet looked like a tiny hovel on the outside. Oh, and the tea shop that wouldn't make any money unless I was eventually allowed to flip over that open sign.

Yes, tomorrow was another day with another adventure.

I had better be prepared.

# Chapter Four

I GLANCED IN the rearview mirror of my Corolla, ignoring the small starburst crack in the corner. A sad sight stared back at me once I was focused on my reflection. My nose was still red, my eyes were still bloodshot, and sadness was written across my features. It was more than evident that I'd spent the morning crying. It had been so hard to say goodbye to Heidi, even though she'd promised to borrow Patrick's car to visit in a couple of weeks.

Those fourteen days were going to feel like an eternity, especially if I couldn't reopen the tea shop after yesterday's incident.

Which was why I was parked in front of the sheriff's office and not the shop. I'd been here for quite a while, considering Heidi's train had such an early departure time. I needed to be assertive in my claim that I be allowed to open the store for business. Besides, I shamelessly wanted to find out exactly who the Fake Larry Butterball was, as well as why he'd targeted me with his shenanigans.

Don't think for a second that it didn't cross my mind that my Nan's will and the ridiculous request that I reside in Paramour Bay for twelve months was just as fake as Larry Butterball was, but I quickly buried that speculation as self-defeating.

I mean, what would I do if that even had a sliver of truth to it? Return to New York City dead broke, where my landlord would no doubt tell me he'd already rented out my one bedroom apartment? I couldn't blame him, though I had promised to send him my back rent as soon as I had time to go over my newfound inheritance.

I sat back in my seat, adjusting the rearview mirror into place. It gave me time to look around the quaint little town. All the regular tourist storefronts had the Norman Rockwell vibe. The cobblestone intersections added to the picturesque scene, as well as the old Gaslamp formed lampposts every twenty feet bearing the town's stylized crest decked out in the season's colors.

Halloween was this Wednesday.

Someone had even gone to the trouble of bundling cornstalks around each and every lamppost. Almost every store had a couple of pumpkins out front with additional decorations. Scared cats, flying bats, and scarecrow silhouettes cut from quarter-inch sheet metal painted black seemed to be a popular choice.

I made a mental note to decorate the shop the same way when Sheriff Drake allowed me back inside the store, not wanting anyone to think I didn't want to partake in the holiday festivities.

A light breeze ruffled the top of the cornstalks, a few loose leaves skipped across the cobblestone crosswalk, and the red light at the second intersection hadn't changed color since I'd been parked alongside the curb. Had I not spied the church's parking lot on my way back into town, I might have assumed everyone had deserted the town in the wake of the recent murder. No one was milling around the sidewalks like they had been yesterday, but there was a good reason for that.

It was only going on eight o'clock on this Sunday morning. The churchgoers were most likely sitting in the pews and listening to the pastor's sermon recounting the wages of sin for the tea-drinking newcomer.

And I didn't even drink tea!

Would there be mention of the town's recent homicide?

I was a bit taken aback when a woman got out of the vehicle parked in front of me. As I'd mentioned before, I had been sitting in my car for over an hour, which meant she'd been doing the same. A bright smile adorned her face, but my eyes were drawn to her hand which she was waving at me as if we were long lost friends from high school.

A quick glance over my shoulder to the sidewalk assured me that this older woman was definitely waving at me and not someone behind my car. I tried my best to smile back, hoping that the redness in my nose and eyes had somewhat dissipated by now.

It wouldn't do me any good to let everyone know that I was about to burst into tears at the departure of my best friend, who had left me in the care of an abnormally tall Colossus, who I still wasn't completely sure was human. Then there was the small inconvenience that I might be a suspect in the town's first murder in a half century.

I've got to tell you, it was becoming a bit overwhelming.

"You must be the lovely Raven Marigold," the woman exclaimed after I'd opened my car door. It wasn't like she'd given me any choice with her headlong rush. She'd walked right up to my Corolla and kept smiling at me until I grabbed my purse and exited the vehicle. Her heavy dose of perfume overpowered the faint scent of bacon coming from Trixie's Diner. "I'm Eileen Weepler. I answered your 911 call yesterday. It's not like we have a big office, so you got me. As a matter of fact, I'm practically on call twenty-four seven. You'll always get me. It's no big deal, really, considering there's hardly any crime to report in Paramour Bay. I just route the lines to my home phone when I'm not here at the office. It's just me and Sheriff Drake. Plenty of room for the both of us. By the way, has he called you this morning? He wanted to talk with you."

I must not be the only one who liked coffee, because Eileen's constant chattering had me thinking the tea shop might benefit her. Maybe I could do some sort of intervention. It might actually be good for business.

"Um, no. I was dropping my friend off at the train station," I explained, wondering how on earth Eileen had managed to slide her hand into the crook of my arm the way she did. She really didn't give me much of a choice but to let her guide me to the glass door of the sheriff's office. I was beginning to wonder if I'd been apprehended. "Why was Sheriff Drake going to call me?"

"Why, he's found out who was pretending to be Larry Butterball," Eileen declared, stepping inside and announcing their presence. "Sheriff, you've got yourself a pretty little visitor this morning. Now, Raven, don't get me wrong. It doesn't make any sense that a man from up north in Wethersfield would be here pretending to be someone he certainly wasn't. Larry is on his way back from his annual vacation in Venice Beach, Florida. So, it's possible he can provide us with some answers once he gets back to town."

"Eileen, I'll take it from here. Thank you."

Sheriff Drake stepped out of his office, wearing pretty much the same type sheriff's uniform as yesterday, with his badge attached above the pocket while the patch was just below the shoulder on the opposite side. His holster was slung low on the right side of his hip, eliciting a smile to my lips as I wondered where his cowboy hat had gotten off to. Eileen's comment about there being little crime in Paramour Bay had me doubting he'd ever drawn his firearm.

My gaze dropped to his left hand out of habit.

I blamed Heidi.

He really was a handsome man, and he was kind about Eileen running on about the case when it really should have been him giving me the update, but he seemed a bit too much of a type A personality for my taste.

"Ms. Marigold, please come into my office. Can I get you anything? A water? Tea, perhaps? Eileen has one of those Keurig machines for the office."

He most likely suggested tea because of my grandmother, but my glands were salivating over the rich aroma of his coffee that permeated the office's air. Would it hurt the shop's business to know that the new owner preferred coffee over tea? Probably. I couldn't bring myself to take that chance, at least not until I knew for certain that my Nan's reputation was in good standing.

"I'm fine, but thank you anyway."

I took in the small desk that was presumably Eileen's, also noting that there was a copier machine, a cute coffee stand sporting her Keurig appliance positioned next to a mini refrigerator, and what appeared to be a bathroom located in the corner. Sheriff Drake's private office appeared to be an addition off the main space.

Eileen had been right.

It was only the two of them seeing to the constabulary need of this town.

That was either a good sign, telling me that they had both been right about the amount of crime in Paramour Bay, or it meant that this local police department was way understaffed, all but forcing them to refer the more serious crimes to either the state police or the county sheriff.

"I should have taken the time to give you my proper condolences yesterday. Your grandmother was a well-respected pillar of the community and a member of the town's chamber of commerce."

I took the well-worn wooden chair available in front of his desk. The other one was filled with numerous papers and files, pushed back into the corner. For a town with little crime, there seemed to be quite a bit of case files in that pile. He was also being overly polite when it came to my grandmother, because his statement had been rather impersonal.

"You didn't like her much, did you?" Remember, I was from New York. I didn't like beating around the bush. "Why is that?"

Sheriff Drake was noticeably taken aback by my bluntness, but someone had been murdered in Nan's shop. I wanted to know why.

While I waited for Liam Drake to decide if he was going to answer me honestly or somehow evade my question altogether, I was able to study his personal domain. There were quite a lot of pictures of him fishing with an older gentleman, as well as one with him and a pretty woman. They were both smiling, but it was easy to tell that she was related to him from the shape of their noses. I was betting on a sister.

The most prominent and extremely surprising wall hanging that told me he was proud of his accomplishments was the graduation certificate from the New York City Police Academy. I had to read it twice, because there was no way the man sitting in front of me was from New York. Everything about him screamed country bumpkin.

"I never said that I disliked Rosemary," Sheriff Drake countered, tentatively taking a seat in the rolling chair so that he was directly across from me. His reaction proved to me that he couldn't have been in New York long. "Your grandmother accomplished a lot during her life here, from the tea shop to establishing the book club at the library. She also hosted several small charities throughout the year, all benefiting our wax museum."

I wanted to ask about the wax museum and the significance it had on this town, but I didn't want to get distracted from my real purpose here. Is that why he'd brought it up? Hoping that I would lose focus on the topic we'd been discussing?

Where was Heidi when I needed her? Oh, that's right. Escaping at lightning speed, the fastest a locomotive could muster. She was on her way to my mother's apartment so that I could call and tell her that I'd left the city without saying goodbye. I would also need to explain why the police were going to be calling her shortly to question her about Fake Larry. I was lucky they hadn't done so already.

I suddenly had a hot flash at what her reaction was likely to be.

"You never said you liked my grandmother, either," I pointed out, proud of myself that I hadn't gotten distracted. I set my purse on the floor beside me before leaning back in the chair so that I appeared at ease. In actuality, I was a nervous wreck about the fact that the man who deceived me ended up dead in my shop. It didn't help my disposition that the killer was still out there. "Look, I'll be honest. I haven't spoken to my grandmother since my eighteenth birthday. I don't know why she left me her tea shop, but I promise you that I will do my best to keep it running until such time that I can sell it without breaking the crazy little clause in her will and default on my obligations. I will also do my best to keep the shop in good standing within the town's usual standards of business."

See?

I could be professional when it was warranted.

Sheriff Drake looked as if he wanted to either swallow his tongue or say something regarding my assurance, which had been quite a feat for me considering I liked to keep to myself. I wasn't the central focus of the party, the way Heidi tended to be. It was probably one of the reasons we got along so well. We kept to our own side of the road. Either way, it would take me awhile to become adjusted to life in a small town.

Of course, there was still the tiny problem of the murder.

"Eileen mentioned that you found out the identity of the man pretending to be Larry Butterball." There was no reason to prolong this visit, especially if I was finally able to get back into the tea shop and get things ready for the grand reopening. I'd never been in charge of anything myself, so a part of me was eager to get started. "What was his name?"

"Jacob Blackleach." Sheriff Drake reached for the lone file on his desk, though I still wondered about the ones in the chair beside me. He flipped open the top cover and turned it to face me. "The state police detective who I called in to take this case ran the victim's fingerprints through the system. He got a hit. Apparently, Jacob Blackleach was from a central Connecticut town called Wethersfield. It's basically north of here, though his surname has no connection with anyone here in town, as far as we know. We're honestly at a loss as to why he'd impersonate Larry, which is why I was going to call you this morning. Are you sure you didn't cross paths with this Blackleach character at any time over the last few months?"

"No." I was absolutely positive I'd never seen the man before. "The first time I'd ever come in contact with him was that first phone call to tell me that my grandmother had passed away."

"Interesting thing about that," Sheriff Drake said, his speculative tone telling me that he had a lot more to share. "Everything Jacob Blackleach told you about your grandmother's last will and testament is completely true."

A part of me sighed in huge relief that I hadn't uprooted my life from the city to come here on a fool's errand. The other part retained the fear I'd experienced upon seeing Blackleach's body, because there still had to be a reason he'd targeted me in the first place.

"Larry—the real Larry—should be pulling into Paramour Bay by this evening. He's driving back from his vacation in Florida to take a look around his office to see if anything is amiss. He knows of only one other person with a key to his workplace, and that's his mother." Sheriff Drake leaned back in his chair as he scooped his coffee cup off his desk. I managed to hold myself back and not snag it out of his hands. "Ms. Marigold, I've got to ask—"

"Raven, please," I requested sincerely, trying not to wince at the way he'd addressed me. It only reminded me of my mother and the fact that I still had to make that dreaded call. "So, what you're basically telling me is that some random conman decided to take over Larry Butterball's business for the day, and I happened to be the sole client he chose to service before an unknown assailant killed him?"

I was so confused as to why and how someone besides my Nan's estate lawyer could have arranged her funeral, as well as a reading of the will, without getting caught. Everyone knew everyone in small towns. Besides, why would someone do that? What did they have to gain by doing any of it?

"That about sums it up, though I'm more concerned with who murdered him. I can only guess it had something to do with Jacob Blackleach deceiving you."

"You don't think that I—"

"No, I don't believe you had anything to do with Blackleach's murder, but that doesn't mean someone else wasn't trying to protect you or the store from this perpetrator. Who else might have known you were coming to Paramour Bay?"

"No one." For some unknown reason, Ted's sunken eyes and wobbly smile materialized in front of me. I shook off the uncertainty that now consumed me. "Not even my mother knows I'm here, though she's about to after I give her a call later today."

"I take it she's not going to approve of you leaving the city?"

Sheriff Drake studied me over the rim of his cup, but what bothered me most was that he put his lips around the edge and tilted the contents until he'd taken a healthy drink of his coffee.

Was that a sparkle of glee in those dark eyes of his?

I resented him in that moment.

"No, she's definitely not going to approve." I had expected to learn a lot more than what Sheriff Drake was sharing with me, and it made me wonder if he wasn't holding some piece of vital information back. "Sheriff Drake, I—"

"Liam." He set his half-empty mug back down on the desk, not bothering to lean forward. His small smile was nothing like Ted's, but I wasn't about to let that distract me. "No one around here really calls me Sheriff other than Eileen, and I think she does it only because she knows it bothers me."

It would be hard for me to call him Liam, because that

would personalize our relationship. He wasn't my friend, and I doubt he ever would be due to me being here for only twelve short months. In all honesty, he'd probably be glad to see me go, seeing as I was the first to report a dead body during his term as sheriff.

"You said that a murder hasn't occurred in the town of Paramour Bay in close to fifty-three years." I'd been watching Liam very closely for any type of sign I was steering the conversation in the right direction. The moment his gaze switched to the files in the chair, I knew I was onto something. "Out of curiosity, did the case have anything to do with my grandmother or the Blackleach family?"

Liam rubbed a hand over his freshly shaven jaw, but I was relatively sure he only did so to buy himself time. My stomach pulled as if someone had set a weight down on my soul. I shouldn't have asked the question, because I wasn't so sure I wanted to hear the answer.

"Yes, Raven."

Wow, that weight wasn't just set down…it was as if it had been dropped from the Empire State Building.

Liam not only gave a reply, but he did one better that had me regretting even coming to Paramour Bay. I definitely shouldn't have accepted that call from the Fake Larry Butterball.

"Your grandmother was a person of interest in the murder of Norman Palmer, whose body was found floating face down in the bay. To the best of my knowledge though, the Blackleach family was not connected to that particular homicide."

# *Chapter Five*

I SPENT THE rest of the morning trying to come to terms with the fact that my dear old Nan might have been a cold-blooded killer, as well as somehow managing to wipe away the dust on every item in the tea shop without breaking a single teacup. It was a miracle in and of itself, made only more so given all the added angst.

I shouldn't have counted my blessings so early, though.

The world often seeks a balance.

"Mom, I'm sorry I didn't tell you before leaving the city." I sometimes use my hands when talking, and I'd gotten a little dramatic when explaining the last three days in meticulous detail repeatedly. And that included finding Fake Larry Butterball dead in the storage room. "Hold on for one second."

I set my cell phone down to pick up the bigger pieces of the teapot that I'd just knocked off one of the high-top display tables. I blamed the purple-haired lady standing across the street for the distraction while flashing her the evil eye. She'd practically materialized out of nowhere and was in the same spot as she was yesterday, though she made no move to enter the store to introduce herself.

Was she waiting for me to flip over the open sign?

Was she a regular, having run out of tea?

I hadn't planned on being open for business for another few

days until I was able to do a little more research, but I also didn't want to miss out on a sale. If the purple-haired lady was one of Nan's customers, wouldn't she be able to tell me what she needed instead of me looking like a complete idiot who didn't know what I was doing?

My cell phone practically vibrated when my mother yelled into her phone.

"I'm here, I'm here."

"You shouldn't have done this, Raven. You need to get in your car and drive back to the city right this minute."

We'd been arguing on and off for the past half hour, with Heidi trying to intervene every now and then in an attempt to calm Regina Marigold down…which was virtually impossible once she got up a good head of steam. In those thirty minutes, she had relatively kept her cool.

Now?

I hadn't expected her reaction to my moving here for twelve months to be quite so dramatic. Yes, I'd expected surprise and possible anger. Even disappointment. But full-blown rage? Her directive was rather harsh, but not the least bit effective.

I'd made my decision, and she would have to come to accept that.

Or not.

"Mom, don't you understand? This is my chance to make something out of my inheritance. I can live rent free in Nan's old house, run her tea shop for one year while I get my head together, and then move back to the city debt free after I check off all the stipulations Nan made in her will. I might be able to even go back to college without working two jobs to pay for my tuition. Having time to study as well as sleep might just have a profound effect on my grades."

"She's right, Miss Regina. This experience will be good for her," Heidi said, her voice coming in loud and clear on the other end of the line. She'd made sure my mother had put the call on speaker phone. I could picture her sitting at my mother's kitchen counter with a glass of wine, even this early in the day. They could both drink me under the table with both hands tied behind their backs. "And we can both visit on the weekends. It won't be so bad. The train ride was quite pleasant. And I'm sure that handsome-looking sheriff will get to the bottom of who killed Fake Larry, the turkey guy."

Okay, maybe Heidi wasn't helping that much, but at least she was there for moral support.

I took the broken pieces of china that I'd picked up off the floor and tossed them in the trashcan behind the register. It had been easy to avoid the back, considering I'd spent most of my time dusting and straightening the delicate items on display. Unfortunately, I now needed a dustpan and a broom.

"You don't understand what you've gotten yourself into there." The beads clicked back and forth as I walked through them. Somehow, my mother's voice rattled even more than those tiny ivory-colored fairies. "You need to get yourself in your vehicle and drive back here immediately. Now, Raven Lattice Marigold."

I was so taken aback to hear my mother use my full name that I totally forgot all about my fear of entering the storage room and being reminded of Larry—I mean, Jacob.

"Mom, I can't do that. I'd lose everything to the wax museum." My mother would come around. I had to believe that she would, because there really was no other option. Besides, Heidi was very persuasive and would no doubt smooth things over once we finally hung up. It did make me wonder why Mom was so desperate to have me leave Paramour Bay. "Is there something I should know about Nan? Does this have anything to do with what happened to Norman Palmer?"

The silence on the line was heavier than the pollution hanging over the streets of New York City after a Friday evening commute.

"It *is* about Norman Palmer," I repeated in shock. My Nan, the same woman who would never play with playdough because it would get underneath her manicured fingernails, might actually have had something to do with a murder. I needed to sit down. Fast. I grabbed the stepladder in the corner, obviously used to reach the higher shelves, and sat on the top step. "Did Nan do him in?"

"What?" Well, it appeared I wasn't the only one appalled at the thought. "Of course, my mother didn't have anything to do with his murder. That is just sheer bollocks."

Boy, it was a good thing I didn't mention that I thought the man might have been my grandfather. That would have definitely sent my mother over the edge.

"Then tell me why you never came back here. Why are there so many secrets regarding our family and this town?"

"Just…just don't go talking to any of those people. I'll be there on Friday, and I'll help you sort this mess out with the lawyer—the real one."

The fact that my mother disconnected the line without saying goodbye told me that she'd worked herself into quite a tizzy. I wasn't too worried that she would show up in Paramour Bay on Friday, for several reasons. I had serious doubts she could muster the courage to make the trip, given that the first one to come to mind was the fact that she hadn't stepped over the town's limit since the day she left. Furthermore, Heidi would have a chance to work her magic.

I sighed and contemplated closing my eyes for just a few moments, but then I realized that I was in the same room where Fake Larry Butterball had been murdered. In all fairness, the state police or their hired minions had done a good job collecting any evidence that might have been part of the investigation.

Then again, it might have been Liam who had gone the extra mile.

The good ol' sheriff was kind enough to let me know that Fake Larry had been hit over his head with a blunt object. It could have easily been one of the many figurines on the shelves. Trust me, I tried to erase the image of the game Clue's classic candlestick from my mind, but it was virtually impossible.

Although it did make me wonder exactly what was used to murder Norman Palmer and how he came to be floating face down in the bay.

It was hard for me to accept that my Nan might have been involved in killing a man, but the fact that she hadn't been arrested told me there had been no proof she'd done anything at all. And it wasn't like it had hurt her business any, because I *had* found one of the financial reports underneath a shelf beneath the register. Surprisingly, this place did do a fairly decent business in various blends of tea.

Now that I'd ventured into the back, I began to look around at all the shelves. There were more glass containers filled with various tea leaves and other herbs, as well as wooden boxes filled with tea sets packed in straw and other fragile items associated with the preparation of the beverage.

Who knew that there were tea chests, strainers, whisks, filters, infusers, and a ton of other accessories that went into making the perfect cup of tea? I was hoping that all this research would give me a taste for the stuff myself.

The many inventory items on hand would certainly help my pocketbook, that's for sure.

Something caught my eye, and it reminded me a lot of the coffee table at my Nan's house. Well, my house. It was very hard to get used to that way of thinking when everything was so new to me.

I stood, pulling my skirt from underneath the small stepladder. I'd gotten in the habit of checking things like that, because as you're aware, I'm not the most graceful woman. Once I made sure I was in the clear, I made my way over to the wooden cabinet that had captured my attention. Sure enough, it had almost the identical carvings as the coffee table in my house.

"Are you back here?"

You know the saying *my heart stopped*? Yeah. That just happened for real.

What happened to the bell above the front door?

The eerie whisper had come out of nowhere, but it was followed by purple hair coming through the off-white beads. The color clash was almost as horrifying as the fact that I'd jumped so far back that I practically knocked over the tiny stepladder.

What was it with people sneaking up on me around here?

"There you are." The shimmering beads began their melodic tune as the older woman slid the rest of her body through the clicking strings. She didn't appear as old up close as she did from far away, maybe having hit seventy, seventy-five at most. One thing was clear, she was just as nervous now as she was yesterday. "I was supposed to pick up my order a few days ago, but I thought it best that I wait."

"I'm sorry," I managed to say in spite of the blood rushing through my ears. My adrenaline was near an all-time high, approaching a new record. Now that I think about it, there hadn't been any part of my recent move that hadn't involved a myriad of emotions. "Your order?"

"Yes, Rosemary assured me that if she should ever pass on to the other side that you would see to it that I was taken care of. It's oh so very important I have it. And my name is Pearl Saffron. I'd stay and talk some more, but I don't want anyone to get the wrong idea with me being here and all."

Wrong idea?

I didn't have a clue as to what Pearl Saffron was talking about, let alone what the wrong idea could be that had her worried. She had the shifty appearance of committing a crime, and for one second, I thought maybe she was responsible for Fake Larry Butterball's death.

Her apprehension was akin to an addict picking up her drug of choice from a new source. But I was talking about a seventy-some year-old woman up against a fifty-some year-old man. There was no way she could have subdued a full-grown male. No, it was doubtful that Purple Pearl had anything to do with Fake Larry's plucking.

"Um, I'm Raven."

I thought I'd start out by introducing myself. It would give me time to try and figure out why Pearl would think I knew something about her order when I hadn't even known my Nan owned a tea shop.

"Oh, I know who you are, dear. Your grandmother, God rest her soul, talked about you all the time." Pearl reached out and patted my hand, but it became clear rather quickly that she had an ulterior motive. She actually slipped me a fifty-dollar bill. "I'll be up front, waiting for my *tea leaves*."

Why had Pearl emphasized *tea leaves* in such a high-pitched tone?

I was left by myself as Pearl made her way back through the strings of beads.

Now what was I supposed to do?

My silent question was answered when a small bag was somehow knocked off one of the top shelves. I confess that in that one moment I considered leaving this shop, this town, and even this city. A miniature paper bag was now lying on its side on the counter with the name *Pearl* written on it in red ink.

It was hard to tear my eyes away from the obvious elephant in the room, but a blur of orange caught my attention. Well, it might have been black. I wasn't sure, but I was almost positive it had fur. I sucked in my breath to steel myself at finding a mouse up on the shelf.

There was nothing there.

Now I began to feel like Heidi. She'd seen something twice, adamant that something had scurried around the shop and my new house. Yet there had been nothing to find upon looking more carefully.

"I'm not going crazy," I whispered to myself, leaning over without taking my eyes off the top shelf. I managed to snag the small paper bag and stand without incident. "I'm not going crazy. I'm not going crazy."

*That's debatable.*

I spun around, certain that someone had actually responded to my mantra, but I was alone in the back room.

Was this it?

Was I going certifiably insane?

Was I hearing voices now?

I no longer wanted to be alone. If that meant talking with Pearl for a while, then that's what I would do. I honestly don't even remember leaving the storage room, but I was through those antique ivory-colored beads before I could hear any more voices inside my head.

"I managed to find your order, Ms. Saffron," I called out, noticing she wasn't browsing or looking inconspicuous in any way. Her eyes had been trained to the magic beads. "At least, I think this is what you've come in for today."

Pearl had already paid me for her purchase, though I still wasn't quite sure what type of tea I was selling her. I decided that being upfront with her was the right choice or else I would have no idea what type of tea leaf concoction she bought on a regular basis.

"Ms. Saffron, I should be honest with you. I'm sure you know that Rosemary hasn't spoken to me or my mother in many years." Pearl's eyes were trained on the brown paper bag in my hand. Again, I refrained from peeking inside. "I don't know anything about the shop. I have a bit of a learning curve ahead of me, but I'm sure I'll get there if you're just patient with me. Are these tea leaves special in some way? Did Nan take a special order from you for some specific company?"

Pearl didn't reply right away, though the lines in her forehead deepened when she frowned her disapproval that I would ask such a question. She held out her hand in impatience.

"Dear, we shouldn't be talking about this here. Anyone could happen to walk inside." Pearl reached forward and took the bag from my hands before lifting the flap of her purse. She carefully set the paper bag inside the opening as if the contents could explode. "Your grandmother was very meticulous in her dealings with me and the others. I'm sure she has a log of some sort hidden away, just as I'm sure you'll pick up where she left off without a hitch."

Dealings?

A log?

Was that in reference to a list of names?

Oh, my!

I was going to be sick to my stomach.

"Ms. Saffron, was my grandmother your drug dealer?"

# Chapter Six

THE IMMEDIATE SKEPTICAL look on Pearl Saffron's face had me questioning my newfound theory that Nan was a drug dealer of some sort. I'm not exactly sure how I could be that far off the mark, given the context of the conversation leading up to this exchange. After all, I'd just given this woman a bag containing a brown leafy substance in exchange for fifty dollars.

"Shame on you," Pearl exclaimed in a huff, closing the flap on her purse with an additional self-satisfied pat. I couldn't understand how I had read the situation wrong, but maybe Pearl wasn't ready to accept the truth herself. If she was spending fifty dollars a week on herbs or tea leaves that were supposed to make her feel good in some way…well, she'd certainly been conned by the best of the best. "Your grandmother would never be involved with any such vice or chicanery, and certainly not that. She all but promised me that you would know what to do in case she passed on to the other side. Didn't she leave you a note or some kind of instructions?"

Could it be that I'd arrived into another dimension when I crossed the county line?

First, the town itself was completely idyllic in every sense of the word. It was as if Paramour Bay was torn off a *Saturday Evening Post* cover. Second, the first murder to have been committed in fifty-three years involved my family. Third, Ted. I mean, just Ted. I don't think I need to go into more detail there.

"In my defense, Ms. Saffron, you're acting like buying tea leaves is a criminal enterprise or some other dubious exchange with malintent." I shouldn't have had to point out the obvious, but we had clearly gotten our wires crossed. It was time to lay all of our cards on the table. "Ms. Saffron, I promise you that I will get this shop up and running to my Nan's standards once I find out what the heck she was doing here. But please, you have to give me a little latitude for misunderstandings. Your order had been previously prepared by Nan. I honestly haven't the foggiest idea what you wanted or what I've just given you. I truly desire to get your order right for next week if I can, but I can't do that if I don't know what type of *tea* you prefer."

I hadn't meant to upset Pearl, but my assurances only seemed to make things worse for her. She was clutching her sapphires and staring at me as if I'd told her that she could never drink tea again.

"Is your son outside?" I asked, remembering the man who'd been with her yesterday outside when a group of people had formed to stand back and watch me walk from my car to the shop. Maybe he could listen to reason and understand that this was all new to me. He might be able to help me convey to Pearl that I couldn't just step into my Nan's shoes as if she'd never died. "Is it possible that I could—"

"Son?" Pearl asked, tilting her head to the side in confusion. Not one purple strand on top of her head moved with the motion. "Oh, darling, I don't have a son."

Pearl snuck a peek toward the door, as if someone was about to barge in and arrest us once the key phrase was exchanged. My gaze reluctantly followed her path. After what she had to say, I'm not so sure that wasn't about to happen.

"This special concoction of herbs is to get Henry Wiegand to fall in love with me." Pearl lifted her shoulders in a sheepish shrug and a satisfied smile. "And it's working quite well! Which is why I needed this week's supply to get him to pop the question."

Oh, this was bad.

Horrible.

Beyond comprehensible.

My Nan had been a conwoman.

I made no qualms that Nan should have been arrested for fraud. Taking money for such a false notion was downright criminal.

What kind of gypsy hocus pocus was this?

I was pretty sure in that exact moment the fifty-dollar bill in my hand began to burn a hole through my palm. Everything began to fall into place...even Fake Larry's murder. He must have been one of her underworld contacts, or maybe even a henchman.

I really should start referring to the man by his real name—Jacob Blackleach.

Had Nan been deceiving Mr. Blackleach, just as she had with the other residents in Paramour Bay? Was it possible to construct a mass delusion so complex that the entire town bought into it? It would certainly explain his murder, especially if Nan had a partner in crime to make sure that certain situations appeared as if they were occurring through some sort of black magic.

Ted immediately sprang to mind as another accomplice.

Yet so did the man I'd mistaken for Pearl's son. She claimed not to have any grown children, yet the bald man who'd been standing next to her...

How did I not make the connection earlier?

I needed to speak with Liam right away.

"Pearl, I'm so sorry that my Nan made you believe that whatever she put in that bag would help you find love. She must have had dementia or suffered from some delusion." I quickly walked over to the counter where I'd left my purse. Don't think I didn't glance at those ivory-colored beads. After all, I most certainly *had* heard someone's voice back there that hadn't been my own. There must be a trap door in the floor or maybe a concealed exit in one of the walls. I could only deal with one crisis at a time, though. "Trust me, no tea leaves or herbs can get a man to fall in love with you. This *is* the twenty-first century, you know."

"But it *is* working, dear," Pearl exclaimed, clutching her purse as if I was going to make an attempt to take it from her. "Rosemary was very special. And she assured me that she passed on her gift to you. I have no doubt."

Gift?

"Well, Nan had a way of making people believe that she could cook, too," I explained, recalling the time she'd ordered from one of the New York's five star restaurants and tried to pass it off as her own creation. My mother had found the warming trays in the trashcan the next day. I couldn't have been more than sixteen at the time, but I can still recall the fight that had ensued over something so meaningless. Nan had insisted that it would end up being a good story to entertain everyone years down the line. No harm was meant. Then again, they had always fought over the simplest of things. "I'm not going to take your money, Ms. Saffron. Go ahead and keep whatever is in the bag, but you'll also take your fifty dollars."

I really didn't give Pearl a chance to try and talk me out of giving her money back, nor did I give her a choice but to walk out the front door with me. There were things I needed to take care of, but first on the list was speaking with Liam about what I'd found out by talking with Pearl. It was essential he know what my grandmother had been involved in, and also that it might very well be in connection with Jacob Blackleach's murder.

"Please come back to the shop should you ever want some actual tea." I certainly didn't want to lose a customer. I managed to give Pearl her fifty dollars back and also lock the door before quickly walking down the sidewalk. I even tossed a wave over my shoulder, grateful that Pearl didn't seem to hold my Nan's deceit against her. "We'll talk soon!"

I looked both ways at the cobblestone crosswalk. Only one car was driving into town, but the man stopped and waited for me cross. I took advantage of his generosity, hastily strolling toward the other side of the road where the sheriff's office was located. To say I was surprised that there was a sign in the door saying they'd gone to lunch was an understatement.

What kind of police department took a lunch break?

Oh, that's right.

The one that employed one sheriff and one dispatcher who forwarded the calls to her home at night.

Well, there was only one place in town that served breakfast, lunch, and dinner. Trixie's Diner was only two storefronts down, so I figured that was my best shot of tracking down Liam. I certainly didn't expect every patron in the place to stop eating and talking the very moment the bell rang over my head, alerting them to my arrival.

You do remember that I don't like being the center of attention, right?

I found it hard to breathe, although I wasn't so certain it had to do with the heavy cloud of grease hanging in the air. It was so silent that I could literally hear the sizzle of the grill through the long rectangular window where the cook was pushing out the finished orders. It was too late to rethink my strategy now, but thankfully, Liam's voice came from somewhere in the back and saved me from what promised to be a very awkward retreat.

Liam was sitting in a booth with an older gentleman, both of them having already finished eating from the looks of their empty plates. I carefully made my way toward them, ever mindful that I didn't brush someone's elbow as they tracked my progress. The last thing I needed was to knock a drink out of someone's hand and cause an even bigger scene.

"Um, I'm so sorry to bother you," I began to say, ignoring the fact that Liam had made room for me in the booth. It wasn't as if I'd come to join them for lunch, and this wasn't a conversation that I felt comfortable having in a room full of residents who had no doubt been conned by my Nan. "I need to speak with you about something important. Well, two things, actually."

"Please, join us." Liam even moved the empty plates closer to the older gentleman, clearly making room for me as he scooted closer to the far window. It was then I remembered seeing this man wearing a policeman's uniform in the framed photograph on the wall in Liam's office. "This is Otis Finley. He was the previous sheriff of Paramour Bay. Otis, this is Raven Marigold."

It was more than apparent that Otis had already been apprised of my identity, for he displayed no surprise at the introduction. My stomach clenched a little at the knowledge that he'd been the previous sheriff. Had he been involved in the case that had determined my Nan was a suspect in a murder? Was that how she'd gotten involved with conning and a flim-flam game of crime to begin with?

Once it was out that Nan had been committing fraud on the good people of Paramour Bay, it wouldn't be such a stretch to believe that she'd go to other extreme measures such as murder and vice.

This so wasn't going to be good for business.

"It's nice to meet you, young lady. I was sorry to hear about the passing of your grandmother. She was a paragon of our community." Otis stood, holding out his weathered hand. It appeared that he still liked to fish from the amount of sun that had touched his skin over the years. It didn't hurt that I saw his fishing hat decorated with various tied flies hooked onto the hatband. It was sitting on the booth beside him, which he was already reaching for in his bid to say goodbye. "I can see that you need to speak to Liam in private, so I'll give you two the table."

"Oh, you don't have to—"

"It's no trouble," Otis assured me with a pat on my shoulder. He even gave me a wink that I found hard to decipher. "I'll be by the shop sometime in the next day or two to pick up my wife's order."

I could only hope that he was talking in the literal sense and not some magic potion. I'm not going to lie. I basically collapsed into the booth wondering if the former sheriff might have been conned by my now dead grandmother.

"Raven, what's wrong?" Liam asked in a low tone after Otis made his way to the cash register. "Did something else happen? Please tell me you didn't find another dead body in the back of your tea shop."

"No, there's not another body. Nothing quite that sinister. That is, other than finding out my grandmother was a con artist." My tone became lower the longer I talked, but it still felt as if every eye in this place had settled onto my back. I slipped my purse strap off my shoulder and shoved my bag into the corner before leaning over the table. At least Liam displayed a sense of humor. That could go a long way in what I was about to divulge about Nan. "Don't get me wrong. It's better than believing that my grandmother was selling drugs to the locals. I think. Either way, I came to tell you that I believe I know who killed Fake Larry. I mean, Jacob Blackleach or whatever his name was."

Was it possible that I had been spending too much time with Heidi?

I needed to get these names straight.

"Who?" Liam seemed skeptical, which wasn't a surprise. He was the sheriff, and I was nothing more than a tea shop owner. It wasn't as if I had police training or had any idea how to crack a murder case. "And we'll get back to your grandmother being a con artist in a second."

"Larry Butterball." It was best I blurt out who I believed to be the guilty party. It would cause this conversation to go a bit faster and maybe diverted to the police station where eavesdropping was limited to Eileen, who wasn't amongst the diners whom I could see when I entered. Maybe she'd gone home for lunch. "Look, the population in Paramour Bay isn't that large. How many bald men could there be around these parts?"

"Technically, four. But that's beside the point." Liam drew his coffee mug across the table as he sat back against the padded seat. It irked me that he didn't seem to take my accusation seriously. "Raven, Larry has been in Florida. He goes to the same resort every year. It's not like that's a well-kept secret. He's not due back until this evening. And I'm not seeing why you would accuse a man who wasn't even in town at the time of the murder."

"But that's exactly what Larry would want you to think, now isn't it?" I wasn't going to sit here and debate something that could be proven in a matter of minutes. "Show me a photograph. I'll be able to tell you if it was him that I saw standing across the street."

"Him, who? You still haven't explained why you believe it was Larry who committed the murder."

"I saw someone outside the shop yesterday before Heidi and I found Jacob Blackleach in the back room. The man in question was standing behind Pearl Saffron. I assumed he was her son, but she told me a little bit ago that she doesn't have any children." This was where I had to explain why I didn't make the connection until now. "The man wasn't quite six feet tall, but he was bald. You mentioned that the real Larry Butterball was bald. What if he found out that Jacob Blackleach was impersonating him? What if he killed Jacob in some crazy criminal enterprise with my grandmother? What if Larry was Rosemary Marigold's partner in crime?"

It was a relief to notice the slight change in Liam's facial expression. He was beginning to take me seriously. Though now that I'd spelled everything out for him, something didn't make sense.

Why would Jacob Blackleach impersonate Larry Butterball? Could Jacob have been an undercover police officer? Or a private detective on some case? The latter made more sense, especially if a relative believed that their mother or grandmother was being conned out of their money by a tea shop owner who claimed she could make love potions out of mixing herbs.

"Give me one moment."

Liam set his mug down on the table with a purpose. He excused himself, walking over to the far wall that contained a ton of framed pictures. It was natural for me to follow his progression, so there was certainly no reason for me to experience shame when the waitress stepped up to the table and cut off my view of that swagger Heidi had mentioned yesterday.

"You must be Raven Marigold." The waitress' nametag read Flo. I had to stare at the plastic rectangle pinned to her uniform to make sure I was seeing those letters correctly. Was everything in this town right out of a dime novel or a television sitcom? To top it off, she literally had red hair, though not worn in a beehive. Her smile instilled fear in me that she'd bought into my grandmother's *herbs* nonsense, too. Were these good people going to persecute me for my Nan's sham? "You're the spitting image of your grandmother. Welcome to Paramour Bay."

"Thank you." I quickly shot a glance around her white apron to see if Liam was heading back this way. He wasn't, so that gave me time to do a little bit of fishing myself. "It's a beautiful town. Did you know my grandmother very well?"

"That woman was a creature of habit," Flo shared with a chuckle. "Rosemary would come in here every day and order the potato soup with a half ham sandwich. She certainly had a…unique…way about her. May she rest in peace."

A cough or two came from the other diners, but Flo waved her hand in their direction.

"Don't you mind them none. They didn't appreciate Rosemary's distinctive personality nor her talents. She was one amazing woman." Flo pointed out the window and toward *Tea, Leaves, & Eves.* "Can I bring you a cup of tea? English, like your grandmother used to love? That reminds me, Trixie made up her monthly order. I believe we're short on the green tea, but I'll bring that list back with your check."

I wasn't thirsty or hungry, but I didn't want to appear rude.

"Yes, a cup of tea would be great," I replied with a forced smile, not wanting anyone to realize that I'd caught onto my Nan's little scheme. "English style, with cream and sugar, please."

If I was going to drink tea, I was going to have to sweeten it so that it at least tasted somewhat like the lattes I preferred back in the city. I eyed Liam's coffee, but decided I best ignore the beautiful, rich java. I had to appear to be a tea drinker if I wanted to sell any, so I might as well start now.

As it stood, I had a lot of ground to make up for.

"I'll make the introductions, seeing as you'll run into quite a lot of these folks." Flo pointed to the counter. "Those two fellas are Albert and Eugene. You'll see them playing chess out front of Monty's Hardware Store most afternoons."

I lifted my hand and gave them a slight wave, wondering if anyone else found this situation as uncomfortable as I did. Here I was, confessing the crimes of my grandmother to the sheriff of Paramour Bay, and the majority of these good people had most likely been her victims.

"Elsie and Wilma are in the first booth. They come here for lunch every Monday, after their hair appointments. Aren't their hairstyles the prettiest things? It's amazing what Candy can do with a blow-dryer and a brush." Flo continued to name the rest of the patrons, even including the couple sitting at the table closest to me. "Desmond and Cora Barnes own the malt shop next door to *Tea, Leaves, & Eves.*"

I couldn't help but notice the grimace that crossed Cora's lips at the mention of my newly acquired shop. I realize that she probably had every right to feel disdain for my grandmother, but

I didn't like the snooty manner in which she showed her contempt.

"We've heard you have to keep the shop open for one year in order to gain ownership. Our lawyer will be in touch with you at that time, seeing as we'd love to expand our space into your lot."

"Cora, let the poor girl order her lunch," Desmond said disapprovingly, his worried gaze skimming over the rest of the diner. He worried about what people thought of him, whereas it was evident that Cora believed others looked up to them because of their obvious station in life. The rings on her hand probably cost more than what I had made for the past three years, maybe even four. "We should be going anyway. We need to be in New Haven by two o'clock."

"Don't mind them." Flo had leaned over the table to collect the empty plates, doing so in order to speak with me privately. I appreciated her support and now understood why Nan had come here for lunch every day. "They're a bit uppity, is all. At least, she is. That's what happens when you come from old money. You begin to believe you're better than the other folks who have lived here just as long. Either way, she still ages with the rest of us."

Had Desmond and Cora figured out Nan's side business? Her obvious dislike for me was disconcerting, seeing as I hadn't been the one to sell anyone a love potion that was probably made of herbs my Nan had gotten out of her own garden. Then again, my grandmother wouldn't have been caught dead pulling weeds in fear of getting dirt underneath her manicured nails.

"This is the real Larry Butterball." Liam had walked up behind Flo, who was now heading around the counter with the empty dishes in her hand. She shot Albert and Eugene a look of warning before she disappeared behind two swinging doors. It was rather difficult to pull my gaze from the two older men, who were now speaking with each other in hushed tones. "Raven? Is this who you saw yesterday?"

A heavy weight settled in my stomach when I had no choice but to accept that I was wrong, at least on the count of who the bald man had been standing behind Pearl.

"No, it wasn't Larry." I sat back in my seat, ignoring the fact that Desmond and Cora had yet to leave their table. The blonde had a grimace to her pink lips that I didn't appreciate, but it did remind me that I had to fess up my grandmother's crimes to Liam. "Liam, I might not know who killed Jacob Blackleach, but I do know that Rosemary has been conning the good people of Paramour Bay."

"I'm sorry?" Liam carefully set down the picture of Larry he'd taken off the wall. "Conning who? Oh, wait. You mentioned that Pearl stopped into the shop this morning, didn't you?"

"Yes." I dragged out the last sound of the word a little bit longer than necessary, experiencing a wave of uneasiness. It was a sensation similar to what I had sensed right before Heidi told me that there had been a dead body in the backroom of the tea shop. "Pearl slipped me a fifty—don't worry, though, I gave it back— and wanted a crazy love potion. Rosemary had some of the residents believing she could concoct magic potions, and she was selling them on the side. I'll go over the books when I have time, but it's pretty obvious she was pocketing the money and not paying any taxes on those ill-gotten proceeds. I'll do my best to assist you in the investigation, but I think it's best for you to speak with Pearl firsthand to—"

"Raven, stop," Liam directed gently, even reaching across the table and resting his warm hand over mine. "Pearl is overly dramatic, but I believe I know what the problem is."

The stark contrast between his touch and Ted's was astounding, reminding me that I hadn't addressed the tenant in my backyard during this conversation. I wasn't able to get another word in edgewise, though, because Liam's next statement had me once again wishing I'd stayed in New York.

"It was public knowledge that your grandmother dabbled in witchcraft. She was the genuine article, if you listen to some folks."

# Chapter Seven

WITCHCRAFT.

My fingers trembled slightly as I slid the key into the slot. I flicked my wrist and was grateful for the solitude the tea shop offered me after that massive bombshell. It was more than apparent that Liam didn't believe in all that hocus pocus, and he'd apparently given Nan a pass on her side business, even allowing Nan and her patrons to revel in their own delusions.

What had Liam called the money that transferred hands?

Oh, that's right.

Donations.

That was like dropping a quarter down a wishing well.

What did it matter if it was donations or payment? Nan was still involved in conning the good residents of Paramour Bay into believing she could make potions that could alter someone's perception or personality.

It was downright criminal to me, like stealing from the donation plate at church.

Honestly, it had taken every ounce of strength I had not to snag the coffee mug in front of Liam, especially before Flo had served me a cup of warm tea. Somehow though, I can now reluctantly admit that the soothing concoction did calm my nerves just a tad bit. There might be more to tea than I had originally suspected, giving me all the more reason to dive into the research I'd been putting off while cleaning the sundry items in the shop.

Should I flip over the open sign or try to figure out Nan's various blends?

I decided to wait until tomorrow, and I made sure to engage the lock so that no one could enter the shop without knocking. The bell seemed to be working perfecting fine now, but Pearl had somehow taken me by surprise earlier. I certainly didn't want another scare like that when I was already on edge.

The scent of lemon hung in the air from my earlier dusting spree, though there was a fruity fragrance mixed in that came from the various tea leaves. It was rather welcoming, and the tension in my shoulders began to subside as I walked over to the counter to hide my purse in one of the cubbies underneath the worktop.

Witchcraft.

Liam hadn't said Wiccan, he'd said witchcraft. Even I understood the difference, but who in this day and age would actually believe in spells and potions?

Nan always had been unique, so it wasn't that much of a stretch to think she used that rather particular image to make a little extra cash. She did have expensive taste back in the day, preferring quality over quantity. She'd obviously hoodwinked Otis into allowing her side business to stay up and running, and Liam must have just followed suit when he'd taken over for sheriff.

If she'd stored Pearl's bag on the top shelve in the storage room, Nan might have done so with others. I wouldn't keep Pearl or those who'd placed their orders from receiving them, but I would ensure that the customers understood that there would be no more future love potions or whatever they might have been looking to change in their lives.

None of this explained why Jacob Blackleach would come to Paramour Bay to impersonate Larry Butterball. I had to wonder if he was part of the con or maybe investigating the witchcraft stories surrounding Nan. Of course, it didn't solve the mystery of who the bald man had been standing behind the gathered crowd yesterday morning, either.

Well, I couldn't do anything about that now. The afternoon was wasting away, and I needed to see who else might be stopping by for their *magical blend* of home remedies. I recalled Pearl's bright smile when she claimed that Henry was falling in love with her all because of the tea or whatever else had been in the bag. At least Nan had made Pearl happy in her later years.

One tended to believe what they needed to when it came to matters of love.

I worked my way through the ivory-colored beads, the musical tune reminding me that I could always use my phone to play some background music. Better yet, maybe I should get those surround sound speakers for the shop.

What kind of music would encourage customers to buy tea?

It was something to think on as I began organizing the numerous small bags lined up on the top shelf of the storage room.

*Lydia.*

*Oliver.*

*Ben.*

*Elsie.*

*Wilma.*

*Otis.*

There were more bags with other names on them, but it just went to show that a lot of the townsfolk in Paramour Bay had come to Nan for something or other. Not all of them were love potions. Otis' bag had instructions on the back, and his magical blend of leaves was intended for arthritis.

I began to feel slightly better, believing that maybe Nan was using tea leaves and herbs as some type of old school homeopathic treatments that were known as those home remedies from the past.

That wasn't so bad, was it?

*Really? Home remedies?*

I'll admit it.

I screamed like a little girl who thought she saw a monster in her closet. Remember, a man was killed right here in this room. Had Jacob Blackleach heard the voice before someone hit him over the head with an object that had yet to be found? Was my time here on this earth about to come to an end?

I hastily spun in a circle, trying to find the person who was talking.

*I give up. At first, it was fun. Now? It's just boring.*

And there, sitting next to those old iron mixing bowls that I'd found so interesting was a…ragged old cat?

Now mind you, I wasn't talking about the average housecat that people had as pets. You know, the ones that purr and weave between your legs to show their love? No. I wasn't even remotely about to describe that kind of cat.

The orange and black furry thing in front of me looked like he'd been put through the wringer and then back again for good measure. A few of his whiskers were bent at odd angles, his left eye appeared slightly larger than his right, and the end of his tail had a crink in it that resembled a bent hanger.

And those weren't the only oddities to stand out once I'd gotten a good look at him.

His fur resembled what a comforter would look like after it

had been washed too many times. You know, where the fabric begins to pill and the material starts to pull? Well, the tuffs of this cat's fur made it seem as if he'd been in the battle of his life.

*I have been, thank you. And I blame your grandmother. Why she left me here to deal with you is beyond me.*

"I've gone crazy," I murmured, wishing I'd brought my phone into the back room with me. I could have called Heidi to come and get me. Maybe Nan was putting psychedelics in her special blends. I didn't feel high, though. I could always have Heidi discreetly sneak me out of town and take me to the nearest hospital. No cat—imaginary or not—should be able to read my mind. I turned around so that I could no longer see it. "I didn't even reach thirty years old before I lost my sanity. I only had three days left."

*I'm not an it. I'm a him. And you may call me Mr. Leo. After all, I was supposed to be a Persian leopard, given my service. Ohhh, I would have been glorious had your grandmother not messed up that darn spell. She didn't listen to me, and now here I am, a leopard stuck in a munchkin housecat's body. Life truly isn't fair.*

He was still talking. I didn't know whether to laugh or cry.

It was then that it hit me. And my understanding would undoubtedly solve Jacob Blackleach's murder. There was a gas leak in the storage room causing hallucinations to those who were exposed to the fumes.

It made perfect sense.

I was hallucinating, and so had Jacob Blackleach. We all assumed that he'd been hit on the head by someone wanting him dead, but what if he'd fainted and hit his head on the corner of the counter on the way down?

*No, he was murdered. That much should be clear.*

"Would you just shut up?" I exclaimed, spinning around and

pointing my finger at a nonexistent cat. "Stop talking. I need to think."

*You need a glass of that wine Heidi left at your house. But alas, so much for getting what we want or need.*

Was the cat supposed to be my subconscious? Did inhaling natural gas cause that type of reaction?

*Not that I'm aware of.*

"How would you know?"

I dragged the stool closer to me so that I could sit down and think this through. I couldn't run back to the diner and tell Liam that I was seeing things or else he might suspect that I was going crazy and actually had something to do with the murder, after all. That left me little choice but to stay here and try to figure things out on my own.

*I could help you with that.*

What could it hurt? Maybe my subconscious had answers that I'd somehow suppressed thus far.

*Let me spell this out for you.*

The cat shimmied his crooked tail until he was in a sitting position, his green eyes focused only on me.

*Rosemary Lattice Marigold was a witch, and so are you, little miss.*

My subconscious was not doing a good job of explaining itself, so I slid my eyes to the strings of ivory-colored fairies. Maybe Liam would go easy on me if I turned myself in to his custody to be committed to a mental institution.

Of course, that would eliminate any chance I had of him asking me out for dinner.

*I wish I could tell you the mental institution was where you belonged, because then my suffering would end. I could then move on to my next incarnation.*

Leo lifted a paw and looked at it lazily as if he wanted to clean himself, but he didn't have the required energy. Or he could have been studying the one claw that was slightly larger than the others. He sighed as if he were dealing with a petulant child.

*But, alas, I cannot lie. You're a witch, and I was chosen to stay behind and teach you the ways of your ancestors.*

"The ways of my ancestors? Obviously, my family has a history of mental issues. That would explain quite a lot, actually." I was making things worse by addressing this strange mirage, but what else could I do? Another thought struck me. "Is Ted even real?"

*Unfortunately, yes.*

Leo licked the side of his paw before stroking his warped whiskers.

*They're a little crooked, not warped. Look, let's move this along, shall we? I'm going to prove to you that I'm not a mirage or your so-called subconscious playing tricks on you. After all, we've got work to do. So go out front to the counter. There's a false bottom in the top drawer. You'll find a ledger with a list of Rosemary's customers inside, along with what spells she used to create the hex bags you found.*

I could have stayed where I was, looking at one of the most unattractive cats I could have ever created with my overactive imagination. But it was best that I get some fresh air. I'd eventually return and see that I'd done nothing more than inhale some gas fumes that had affected me in an odd way.

Yes, that was the best course of action.

I practically dove headfirst through the string of beads. I had every intention of heading straight for the door to breathe in the coastal breeze until I was thinking clearly. After that, I'd place a call to the gas company.

But something stopped me.

*A false bottom in the top drawer.*

That's what the cat had said, and as peculiar as that might sound, it would be easy enough to disprove. I tentatively took the last few steps until I was standing behind the cash register. I'd already looked inside the drawer earlier when I'd been dusting and rearranging things to suit my specifications. I hadn't seen anything unusual. But what could it hurt to check, right?

I ever so slowly pulled on the knob, which was silly. It wasn't as if a snake was going to jump out and bite me. Then again, who knew at this point what my overactive imagination could come up with, but an odd-looking cat was totally different than a slimy reptile.

It didn't take me long to pull out the pens and papers from inside the drawer. With a little manipulation and a lot of disbelief, I discovered the false bottom. It was right there like he'd said.

A few realities hit me in that moment, but only one stood out glaringly amongst all the others.

I was a witch.

Don't get me wrong. I didn't feel like a witch, pointy hat and all. I didn't have a wart on the end of my nose and my skin wasn't green. I couldn't wiggle my nose and have someone disappear, no matter how many times I may have wanted that to happen. Honestly, I've never done anything in my entire life to ever indicate I had any kind of powers other than inhale caffeine at a rapid pace.

*That's a misnomer. A true witch can't wiggle her nose and make some poor sod disappear.*

Leo had come out of nowhere. I'd left him in the back room,

and he suddenly appeared next to the cash register.

*I, on the other hand, can disappear anytime I want. I figure we have two minutes before the Bobbsey twins make their way across the street, so I'll make this quick. You devise power from the earth. At first, Rosemary believed you would come into your gift at eighteen. It was the reason she'd gone to visit you in the city on your eighteenth birthday. When you showed no signs of connecting with the source of your power, she left you and your mother to live your lives in New York. It wasn't until a few years ago that she'd discovered there was a second occasion in a witch's natural life where a witch's powers can be harnessed inside her body at the age of thirty. If your family lineage follows the same pattern as before, you—*

I admit, I was so caught up in Leo's explanation that I was surprised when he stopped speaking.

*What was I saying?*

"Seriously?" Was Leo toying with me? I wouldn't put it past this particular imaginary cat, especially seeing as I still wasn't one hundred percent sure that he wasn't a figment of my imagination. "You were talking about my family's lineage and something about there being a pattern from before. My thirtieth birthday is in three days."

If I wasn't going certifiably mad, then Leo the cat might actually be telling me the truth.

*It's Mr. Leo to you.*

The cat's whiskers twitched in irritation.

*I know I'm speaking with a novice, but surely you've watched enough television shows to know that a familiar dies alongside his or her patron. I shouldn't even be here. I've got a few more reincarnations to go. But no, Rosemary wouldn't listen to reason, and now I'm stuck with you. I could be in my new glorious self, catching all the bigger game and reigning like the king I am on the other side of the rainbow bridge. It's an atrocity, is what it really is.*

"I don't understand." The thing of it was, having a conversation with a cat who could appear and disappear at will was becoming rather normal in the short timespan that I'd discovered him. "What did Nan do to you?"

*Rosemary knew that you had no one to show you the way forward, seeing as your mother cast aside her gifts. She had no choice but to leave someone or something behind to help you out. That someone was me, although any spell that goes against the balance of the good in nature comes with a price.*

Leo shot an irritating glance at his tail before continuing.

*My glorious self somehow became this...this so-called fur bag. Oh, and short term memory loss came with the consequences. It's not like I'm this way normally. Speaking of which, I'm sure I'm forgetting something.*

A knock came at the glass door.

*Ah. The Bobbsey twins. They'll want their hex bags. We'll have to continue this later, but there is something you should know—never disclose your true gift. To anyone. These half-wits believed that Rosemary dabbled into witchcraft, and thereby could somehow grant their wishes. Dabbling in witchcraft is something entirely different from being a true practitioner.*

And just like that, Leo was gone. He'd vanished into thin air as quickly as he'd appeared.

*A true practitioner.*

A witch.

That's how Leo had referred to me. I glanced down at the ledger with its intricate carved leather and the astounding secrets that it no doubt held. I'd seen the symbol somewhere before, but I couldn't place it. Unfortunately, my curiosity would have to wait, but at least my hysteria had somewhat subsided for the moment.

Again, my acceptance of such an encounter had me questioning on whether or not I'd completely lost my sanity by thinking this was a normal occurrence in someone's life.

Another knock resounded firmly throughout the small shop, reminding me that I needed to appear somewhat composed. I quickly put the false bottom back in the drawer before swiping all the contents off the counter and back inside. Leo's warning had come across loud and clear, though I wasn't so sure of what the consequences would be if someone discovered that Nan had truly been a witch. Or that I was a witch.

Was I?

"Coming," I called out, shutting the drawer and making my way around the counter. I smoothed my skirt down with trembling and sweaty hands. Would these ladies buy that I was still upset that a man had been murdered in my shop? That wasn't so unreasonable, now was it? It didn't take me long to flip the lock and open the glass door. "I'm so sorry, ladies. I'm technically still closed until I can get the tea shop ready for business, but Nan left behind some paperwork that indicates I have something for you. Please, come in."

"We didn't get a chance to talk to you over at the diner, but we wanted to let you know how sorry we are at Rosemary's passing," Elsie said, handing over a small plate of croissants from the bakery next to the diner. "We noticed you didn't eat lunch with Liam, so we thought we'd bring you something that had some substance."

"And we also wanted you to know that you shouldn't worry your pretty little head over that Cora Barnes. She and her husband have been trying to get Rosemary to move her shop down the street to the vacant spot that has been up for lease...how long has it been now, Elsie? A year now?" Wilma frowned in distaste when she glanced out the display window. "Cora and Desmond have been trying to do the same thing with Mindy Walsh. She owns the adorable boutique on the other side of the malt shop, if you didn't know that already."

"Speaking of which, you and Mindy are about the same age. Wilma, we should introduce them."

I'd noticed at the diner that these two older women talked somewhat constantly, hardly allowing anyone else to get a word in edgewise. Believe it or not, their talkative manner actually eased my nerves that I had a somewhat bereft sarcastic cat in the back room who fully believed he had been meant to be a Persian leopard in this life or the next.

That wasn't the crazy part.

I was beginning to truly believe that I wasn't insane, and that Leo—

*Mr. Leo to you.*

I spun around, thinking maybe he actually had the audacity to show himself, but he was nowhere to be found.

*I don't look that bad.*

I would have responded to Leo, but I caught myself just in time. Instead, I addressed the women and told them it wouldn't take me long to find their order before proceeding to the back of the shop.

"Would you stop talking to me when I'm in front of people?" I chastised Leo once I was through the strings of fairies. I brought myself up short, looking back at the carved beads. Now things were starting to make sense. "It's true, isn't it?"

*And she wins a prize.*

I decided not to respond to Leo's mockery, because that would only further entice him to continue on the path that would no doubt lead to his demise at my still innocent hands. He was sitting next to the bags that he'd somehow gotten to fall from the top shelf. Both Elsie and Wilma had orders with their names on them.

This time, I couldn't resist. I opened one of them and peered inside.

*They're called hex bags. Not all of Rosemary's clients get them, though. It depends on the client's needs. Pearl uses a mixture of herbs to give to Harold in his tea, thus causing him to have feelings for her. The hex bags are something else entirely, but I'll have to explain those to you in detail at a later date. Your customers are waiting.*

Leo yawned, showing his crooked fang. I had so many questions I needed answers to, but he was right. Now wasn't the time.

"Leo, don't you dare disappear on me," I warned him in a soft voice, grabbing the bags and heading for the strings of fairies. "We're closing the shop early, heading home, and then you're coming clean about *everything*. And that includes Ted, the giant whatever living in my backyard. Oh, and you were right about me needing that wine."

I pasted a smile on my face as I maneuvered my way through the various high-top tables, noting right away that Elsie and Wilma were whispering like two young schoolgirls gossiping about the new girl in town. They were most likely wondering if I'd continue to follow in my grandmother's footsteps with regard to their orders.

What had Leo alleged earlier? There was a major difference between this town believing my Nan had dabbled in witchcraft and them having full knowledge of her being a witch. And the same would go for me, if any of his ramblings even held a morsel of truth.

A part of me was still leaning toward a gas leak, but that wouldn't explain the fact that I knew the exact location of my grandmother's ledger in the false bottom of a specific drawer. Leo had also mentioned a spell book, but that hadn't been with the ledger.

"We can't tell you how happy we are that you'll be taking over the shop," Elsie said, solidifying my opinion that she was the lead ringer out of the two. Wilma followed along, though it was evident that her hazel eyes observed anything and everything within her sight. "We were so afraid that the recent murder would run you out of town."

Jacob Blackleach.

It still seemed surreal to me that it was only yesterday morning that Heidi and I found his dead body in the back of the tea shop. There had been a lot of strange things happening around me lately, but everything was starting to make sense now that Leo had made an appearance.

Magic was real, after all.

Was Jacob's name listed in the ledger? Had he been one of my grandmother's clients?

Leo had mentioned that Jacob's death had been murder, which meant he must know the identity of the guilty party.

"We'll see you next week, dear."

"I'll do my best to have everything ready for you," I replied with confidence, totally unsure of any such assurance. Leo said he was here to teach me what my Nan couldn't, but there was still a slight chance I'd either gone insane or inhaled gas from some leak in the old building. I'd know soon enough, because I planned on asking Leo who killed Jacob Blackleach the first chance I got. "You have a good afternoon, ladies."

*You know, we apparently got off on the wrong foot. It's* Mr.

Leo. *Mister, being the key word here.*

The ruffian cat had suddenly materialized by my side, taking his time observing the window shoppers as some of the towns-folk took advantage of the beautiful fall day.

*I think I'll take a sunbath while you drive.*

"You'll do no such thing," I said as I left him at the door to go and gather the ledger. I quickly made my way over to the counter before pulling the drawer open and repeating the same steps I had before in order to locate the leather-bound book. I planned to take it home with me and see who all had been my Nan's clients from Paramour Bay. "First, you're going to tell me who murdered Jacob Blackleach. I'll come up with some way to tell Liam so that he can make an arrest. It's best he doesn't know anything about you."

I took the brown silk ribbon that bookmarked one of the pages in between my finger and thumb, pulling on it to reveal the last date my grandmother had wrote in the ledger. It happened to be the morning of the day she'd died. Out of the blue, a cold draft came down from the ceiling and was the cause of my goosebumps.

"Leo?" I wasn't about to get sidetracked about the shop's air conditioning. It was getting to be that time of year where I'd have to shut it off anyway, preparing for a cool autumn. "Who killed Jacob Blackleach?"

*Well, I remember watching him go through all the shelves in the back. He was looking for something, and then...*

"Then?" I glanced up to find Leo's whiskers even more warped than before, if that were even possible. It might have been his thinking face, but I couldn't be sure given the slight lift of his top lip from the crooked tooth. "What happened then, Leo?"

*Funny thing about that,* Leo said rather nonchalantly, swishing his bent tail from side to side as he made his way toward me. *Did I mention that I have short term memory loss? It's rather unfortunate, really.*

## Chapter Eight

"**C**AN I HELP you with something?"

The back of my head hit the steering wheel as the monotone voice came out of nowhere.

"Owww." I rubbed the spot where there was sure to be a goose egg shortly before crawling out from the floor of my car. "Ted, you have to stop doing that kind of stuff."

"Offering you my help?"

I sighed as the pain began to somewhat recede, but it honestly just blended in with my previous headache. And it was a doozy.

"Is that such a horrible thing?" Ted asked when I didn't respond to his previous question.

Who wouldn't have a headache under these insane circumstances?

I had discovered earlier today that my Nan was a witch. No, she was an honest to God, boil you in a potion kind of sorceress. Her former familiar was bound to this plane of existence in the form of a Persian leopard trapped in a munchkin cat's body. He had been left with a myriad of other physical problems, including short term memory loss. On top of all that, it would appear that I was no closer to finding out who killed Jacob Blackleach than I was yesterday.

Today wasn't shaping up to be the best day of my new life as a self-employed small business owner, that's for sure.

I sat in the driver's seat of my car to face Ted, who had somehow once again been able to sneak up on me without the slightest sound. It was downright creepy, and I had to wonder if Nan hadn't given him a spell, potion, or hex bag to grant him such an annoying trait.

"I was talking about how quiet you are, Ted." I finally lowered my hand in defeat, believing I had no choice but to drive back into town. "I lost my phone. I could have sworn I had it with me when I left the shop, but it's not in my purse."

"Do you have pockets that you might check?"

Okay, Ted's sincerity was rather endearing.

"No, I don't have any pockets, but that was a good suggestion." A thought crossed my mind. "Ted, would you like to drive into town with me? I don't see another vehicle here, so I'm assuming you don't have one. If you ever need a lift, all you have to do is ask. I have to go back into town, because the only place I could have left my phone was at the tea shop."

"I'd like that."

Without another word, Ted began to walk around the front of the Corolla. My gaze happened to land on the living room window, where Leo was poised and cleaning his odd-colored fur. His relaxed stance made me wonder if he hadn't had something to do with my missing phone.

Leo had mentioned he could hear my thoughts. Most of my contemplations were centered on calling Heidi, needing the reassurance that I wasn't losing my mind. I needed a dose of reality, and she was my only tether left to my former world.

You're probably wondering why that wouldn't be my mother, but what if for some crazy reason she confirmed every insane thing that had happened today? I couldn't take that chance. Not right now. I needed more time to accept these outrageous illusions and claims made by a talking cat asserting to be a leopard.

"Here," I said after Ted opened the passenger side door, "let me slide the seat back."

Ted was tall enough that I wasn't so sure he would fit inside my car, but he somehow managed to fold his legs and tuck his body in such a way that he could close the door. Visions of those funny cartoons broadcasted on Sunday morning came to mind, but they immediately vanished when he waved toward the house.

I quickly looked back at the window to find that Leo had stopped cleaning his fur and was looking directly our way.

"You can see Leo? The cat?"

"Of course."

Ted looked directly ahead as if I'd already started the car and we were on our way into town. His short replies were rather irritating, but I gathered my patience as I thought back over the last couple of days. I might not be that crazy, after all.

"Can everyone see Leo?"

"Yes, when he wants them to."

I almost asked Ted if everyone could see all close to seven feet of him, but that question had already been answered by Heidi herself. She'd seen and spoken to Ted. She'd also seen something furry twice, once at the store and the other inside the house. Ted had confirmed that Leo existed, and the ledger all but proved everything Leo had shared with me this afternoon.

So it was true, beyond a shadow of a doubt.

I was a novice witch.

Right?

"Ted, was Rosemary Marigold a witch?"

"Yes." Ted shifted in his seat, sparing a glance toward my

still open door. I couldn't tell if it was in unease or if he truly was adjusting his large frame against the small seat. "Are we going to drive into town? I'd dearly like to be back before nightfall, if at all possible."

Those were the most words Ted had strung together since I'd met him, but it was his answer that had me finally accepting reality.

Sort of.

"I don't feel like a witch." I had no choice but to close my door and start the engine if I wanted to get ahold of my phone any time in the near future. Besides, Ted was getting fidgety. Plus, this was my chance to get some answers. I had him all but trapped inside a small confined area. He had nowhere to go. I wasn't sure what to ask first, so I drove slow and asked the obvious. "Ted, how long have you known my grandmother?"

"Oh, going on ten years now."

Ted looked out the window as I drove the car past the Paramour Bay population sign. It wasn't made of metal like the ones in New York. This welcome post was made of wood and painted in nautical colors. The white portion of the wood had noticeably chipped, but the navy-blue numbers looked fresh.

Ted said nothing more as I lifted my foot off the gas pedal. With his short answers, I was going to have to quicken my pace of asking just the right questions to elicit the responses I needed.

"Have you always lived on her property since moving to Paramour Bay? Are you the caretaker?"

"Yes."

"To both questions?"

"Yes."

"And Leo is real?"

"Mr. Leo is certainly very real," Ted exclaimed with a sideways look, injecting a bit of defense into his monotone voice. He'd taken offense to my inquiry, but it was the title he'd given to the cat that caused me to smile. "The type of spell Rosemary used came with strings, as all types of magic does."

"Do you mean *black* magic?" I was getting off course, but even I'd watched enough movies to know that black magic was very, very bad. Wait. Fake Larry, aka Jacob Blackleach, had called Nan a wicked witch. "Was my grandmother a bad person?"

"Oh, goodness no. Not at all." It was hard to keep my eyes on the road when Ted was actually making facial expressions. His sunken cheekbones made it virtually impossible to know what he was thinking, but every now and then his thoughts came through loud and clear. "Rosemary did what had to be done to continue your family legacy."

Once again, pieces of information were starting to fall into place. Leo mentioned that when a witch died…so did his or her familiar. At least, that was the party line. Yet Nan had cast a spell of sorts to ensure Leo remained behind to show me the way. A warm, tingly sensation washed through my body at finally accepting that Nan had loved me and my mother.

"Ted, what about my mother?"

"Regina wanted no part in the supernatural."

Ted reached out quickly and rested his hand against the dashboard. I quickly pressed on the brakes as we came up to the first intersection, pretending I'd known all along that the stop sign was there. The next street over was the tea shop, but I didn't want this conversation to end.

"So, you're saying that my mother is fully aware that Rosemary was a real witch," I commented, waiting for Ted to confirm my suspicions. His curt nod told me exactly what he thought of my mother, but he certainly wasn't the only one. She had a tendency to have that effect on people. So much of this was beginning to make sense to me now, and all I wanted was my phone so that I could call Heidi and tell her what had transpired today. There was one more thing I needed to know before I parked the car. "Ted, does Leo have short term memory loss or is it an act? Because he told me that Jacob Blackleach really was murdered, but Leo claims he doesn't remember the identity of the killer. That doesn't make any sense to me."

"Rosemary used a spell to prevent her familiar from dying a natural death. Mr. Leo suffered as a result of that type of necromancy magic." Ted looked out the passenger side window. "How much time do I have to run my errand?"

I frowned when I realized we had already arrived back at the tea shop. It was going on six o'clock in the evening, because Leo and I hadn't left the shop when I'd wanted to after Elsie and Wilma's visit. I had too many things to take care of in light of the upcoming sales, such as typing in the dates and times on my phone to keep track of the orders the customers would be picking up within the next week.

Surprisingly, there were quite a few parking spots open on my side of the street. The other side of the road was pretty much full of vehicles owned by the patrons eating their last meal of the day at the diner. It was too bad I couldn't continue driving through town, though, seeing that I'd only had a handful of questions answered. I should be grateful that Ted had spoken full three sentences before letting him out of the car.

"You can take however long you need to, Ted," I offered, not wanting him to feel rushed when I was the one who had extended the offer to bring him into town. Besides, I got to drive him back home. I finished parking and turned off the engine.

"Just come back to the tea shop when you're done. I'm going to go inside and find my phone so I can make a few calls back to New York."

Ted's blue eyes darted around the somewhat empty sidewalks, causing me to think that maybe it hadn't been a good idea to bring him along. He certainly wasn't of average size and definitely stood out as being different. Was he worried what people would think of him? Did he not come into town often?

"What is it you need to do? I can tag along with you, if you'd like. I can make my calls later."

Why I suddenly felt so protective of Ted was beyond me, but for some reason, he'd been close to my grandmother. In a way, it was almost as if she wanted someone to be here in order to take care of him, and I couldn't imagine that responsibility being left to Leo. After all, he couldn't even recall what happened yesterday morning with Jacob Blackleach. I gathered my keys and purse while waiting patiently for Ted to make a decision.

"I do not need any help, but thank you."

Ted's formality was no longer hard to decipher. It was a part of his personality, and I found myself being endeared to his innocent nature. His cold hand patted mine as if to stress how appreciative he was of my offer.

I stayed in the car while he took his time unfolding his large frame, even watching him walk away after he'd closed the passenger door. To my surprise, he didn't get far or even go to the small grocery store located a few blocks down. Instead, he entered the boutique that Elsie and Wilma mentioned earlier.

I recalled them saying a woman by the name of Mindy Walsh owned the quaint clothing and jewelry store.

What would Ted be doing in there?

I hate to admit this, but the hard knock that banged against my window happened so suddenly that I screamed aloud. Déjà vu hit me like a tractor trailer rig. My keys landed somewhere on the passenger side floor, but I managed to catch my purse before it could slide off my lap.

"Sorry," a muffled apology came through the window. Liam stood there with a healthier and younger looking Fake Larry. Okay, technically, the real Larry looked nothing like Jacob Blackleach. And neither one of those men had anything on Liam. "Do you have a moment?"

I quickly fished my keys off the dirty mat, but kept them in my hand instead of shoving them inside my purse. It would be easier to speak inside the tea shop instead of outside on the sidewalk. The weather in the evenings was becoming rather chilly, and I hadn't brought a jacket with me. I only had a sweater in the back seat of my car.

"Raven, this is Larry Butterball," Liam said after the two men had backed away from the car so that I could open my door. I closed it behind me before extending my arm with a half-smile that hopefully conveyed how sorry I was that Larry had to cut his vacation short. "Larry, this is Raven."

"I'm sure you hear this a lot, but you are the spitting image of your grandmother. She and I used to have the most entertaining conversations over her estate, and I'm truly sorry for your recent loss."

For once, someone seemed rather genuine in expressing their condolences.

"Thank you, Mr. Butterball. It's so nice to meet you," I conveyed sincerely as I heartily shook his hand. He was alive and not guilty of murder. That's what mattered most, especially to those residents here in town. "I have so many questions for you, but I am truly sorry that you got mixed up with this matter."

"Have you eaten?" Liam asked with a gesture toward the diner. There was no hint of recognition that I'd driven into town with Ted, but for some reason, I could sense that he'd seen the large man enter the boutique. Was this the type of witchcraft Leo had spoken of when denying that a twitch of a nose could move items or make people disappear? It was very hard to get that particular television show out of my head when thinking of witches. "Larry drove straight through the last eight hours, so I suspect he could use a meal."

"I wish I could, but I drove Ted into town so he could run an errand. I also left my cell phone inside the tea shop." Honestly, the questions I had were rather personal and regarded my grandmother's will in spite of Liam disclosing that Jacob Blackleach had been telling me the truth regarding the stipulations. Still, it couldn't hurt to confirm the details with Nan's estate lawyer. "Do you mind coming inside with me?"

"Of course not," Larry replied, moving back another step so that I could lead the way. Ted had still not materialized from the boutique, and my curiosity began to grow as to why he'd gone inside. Did he know Mindy? "Liam caught me up to speed with what happened here, and I can't believe you were on the receiving end of whatever con Jacob Blackleach was running here. I've never met the man before, and I have no idea how he got the key to my office in order to have access to your grandmother's paperwork. We're a pretty small town where this kind of thing never happens to anyone, so you can imagine that we're all still in a bit of shock."

Liam held open the door for us after I'd unlocked the deadbolt, but I didn't miss the way his gaze observed the interior of the store. I hadn't asked him if he'd learned anything else from the state police detective who was leading the investigation, but I doubted they would find out anything to aid them in solving this case. Something inside of me was screaming that Jacob Blackleach's death had everything to do with my grandmother being a witch.

Every time I even thought of the word *witch*, I had to stop myself from either laughing out loud or driving to the nearest hospital so they could lock me away in a padded cell. Yet with each passing second that ticked by on the antique clock over the cash register, I truly believed Leo was real and that he was telling the truth.

"Do the two of you know Ted?"

I threw out that question just to ease my curiosity.

"We've met a few times," Larry replied with a shrug. "He would accompany your grandmother into the office every now and then when she wanted to update her will...which was more often than you might think."

Often?

"I spoke with Detective Swanson around an hour ago." Liam pulled my attention away from Larry. Both of them had followed me over to the counter where my phone should have been next to the cash register. But it was gone. Vanished. How was that even possible? "There are still no new leads as to why Jacob Blackleach would con you into believing that he was Larry. The detective did speak with your mother, though, and she confirmed everything in your statement."

Maybe it was a good thing I couldn't find my phone. There was no doubt in my mind that my mother had tried to call me a hundred times since her phone conversation with the good detective.

"Believe it or not, Detective Swanson thinks Blackleach's criminal actions might have to do with me," Larry confessed, shaking his head slowly in confusion. The overhead light of the shop glistened off his head, reminding me of the Mr. Clean commercials. "My ex-wife's family was from Wethersfield, but she claims not to know this Jacob Blackleach."

"And no one has claimed his body from the morgue."

"Paramour Bay has a morgue?" I asked, opening the drawer where Nan had kept her journal. There was a chance I'd slid my phone inside with the other papers after I'd retrieved the ledger, but I had no such luck in finding my lifeline to Heidi. "And what will happen to Jacob Blackleach's body if no one claims it?"

"The county has a morgue located in New Haven." Liam was watching me rather closely as I closed the drawer and began looking in the cubbyhole underneath the counter. "The body will be kept anywhere from three to six months. If no one claims the deceased, Jacob Blackleach's body will be cremated and his remains given to a local pauper's cemetery."

"Could we meet tomorrow morning at my office to go over your grandmother's estate?" Larry asked, having joined me in my search for my phone. That was very thoughtful of him. I could see why someone so willing to help with something so mundane would be willing to handle estates. "Though it sounds like you've been given the right information regarding the stipulations in your grandmother's will, it's best we go over them together to be certain. Raven, are you sure you left your cell phone here? I don't see it lying around."

Neither did I, and that was a problem.

"I don't either, but I suppose I could have dropped my phone in between the seats in my car." I glanced out the display window, but I wasn't quite ready to end this conversation. I decided to address something else that was bothering me, though I was very careful how I worded my inquiry to Liam. "I know we discussed my grandmother receiving *donations* for tea blends she believed could help her customers in various ailments and such, but how can you be sure Jacob Blackleach wasn't killed because of that? I still find it odd that she would do such a thing."

"I don't know about Liam, but I can personally vouch for Rosemary's special tea blends." Larry had stopped searching when I mentioned that I could have left my cell phone in the car, so he leaned a forearm against the counter with a smile. It was obvious that he'd been an actual client of Nan's and had no idea the truth behind those *blends* or that she'd gotten them to work because of magic. "I had the worst case of athlete's foot. Nothing I used over the counter from the pharmacy was working, so she had me drink her special tea for five days and voila! Poof. Gone. A total miracle. Your grandmother really knew her herbs."

It was obvious that Liam wasn't totally convinced that Nan was simply a faith healer of some sort, but he remained silent as he glanced over at the string of beaded fairies. I didn't want him to think I was hiding anything, so I crossed the room under the pretense that I was going to look for my cell phone in the back.

I encouraged both of them to join me.

"You know, she left me some of her recipes," I shared willingly over the melodic clicks as the strings moved in time with our entrance. Leo was nowhere to be found, but then again, I'd seen him in the living room window of my house. I wasn't quite sure how he appeared and then disappeared at will, but I'm sure I was bound to find out in the near future. "Pearl was by the shop earlier today, and I had to all but promise her I'd continue to make her the blend she'd been using on Harold...not that I believe she can force Harold to fall in love with her. Now your athlete's foot is another story, because I've read about the antioxidants in teas and how good they can be for a person's body."

I gagged a bit thinking about Larry's feet, but I still managed to keep a straight face. I was more concerned in convincing Liam that Nan hadn't been a witch. Leo was right in saying that dabbling in witchcraft was extremely different than harnessing supernatural powers. Yet I felt no different than I had before, which had me questioning if maybe I hadn't fallen into Rosemary's footsteps.

Could I be the end of a lineage that had apparently gone on for decades?

What if my mother was the last branch in the family tree?

"I don't see your phone in here, either," Larry said, having moved some things around a bit. Neither he nor Liam appeared that concerned with the cast iron mortars and grinders on the shelves. And yes, I did do a bit of research on that this afternoon, as well. A mortar and pestle are those medicine bowls used to grind herbs, spices, and various other items into powder. "Looks like it's probably in your car somewhere."

Larry exited the room first, entering the main shop while leaving Liam behind with me. I didn't think anything of it until I'd gone to follow and found him staring at me in the same manner in which Patrick looked at Heidi.

The half-smile did a number on my heartrate.

"You intrigue me, Raven Lattice Marigold."

And he used my full name, which somehow released butterflies into my stomach.

My reaction was totally different than when my mother said those three words together.

"And why is that?" I asked, tilting my chin slightly higher so I could see his reaction to my question. It was kind of fun to watch his brown eyes darken with interest. "Because the majority of the town thinks my grandmother was a witch, and that I might follow in her footsteps?"

The shooting pain on the side of my knee prevented Liam from answering me.

"Ow!"

I quickly leaned down to see the damage, immediately guessing what had taken place after lifting my skirt and seeing the surface scratches on the side of my leg. Leo had finally made an appearance, and he didn't like me talking about Nan being a witch.

Ouch!

Leo most likely would have swiped at my ankle, but I currently had on my favorite pair of black boots.

"Are you okay?" Liam asked with concern, closing the distance between us to see what I was looking at underneath my skirt. I quickly dropped the colorful fabric and stood, bringing him up short. Were his lips as soft as they looked? "What happened?"

"Oh, my knee acts up every now and then." I had no choice but to tell that little white lie, or else Liam would most likely have me in the back of his police car on the way to a psychiatrist. I did wonder if Paramour Bay had one of those on hand, but thought it best to lure Liam out of the back room before anything else happened that I was unable to explain. "Oh, just an old motorcycle injury."

"You ride motorcycles?"

Well, I was certainly digging myself a hole, wasn't I?

"No, not anymore," I hedged, thinking back to those few dates with a wilder set of boys I tried everything under the sun to forget now. Larry was waiting for us, and it was more than apparent he was anxious to go eat that dinner he'd mentioned earlier. "Larry, does nine o'clock sound good to meet with you at your office tomorrow?"

"I usually met with Rosemary before she had to open the shop, so eight o'clock is fine if you're game. I wouldn't want to put you out."

Larry had pointed toward the door where the times of the shop had been hand-painted in yellowish-gold paint to match the storefront name.

"I haven't officially opened the store. I was thinking of having a grand reopening in a couple of days, seeing as Wednesday is Halloween and everyone will be in town for the trick or treating event at all the shops. By the way, Liam, I think it's a great idea for the town to host that type of—" I had walked over to the counter to gather my purse, coming up short when I saw my cell phone. "How in the—"

*You can't tell Heidi the truth…or anyone else, for that matter.*

Leo *was* in attendance, but he'd been wise to stay out of sight. I can't believe that he'd been the one to have my phone this entire time. It wasn't like he could use his claws to carry it around or anything like that.

*I have my ways. Oh, and your mother called approximately eight times. You might want to call her back before she shows up on your doorstep earlier than Friday morning.*

"Raven, are you sure everything is okay?"

Liam's concern was touching. I wanted nothing more than to shout from the rooftops that I was a witch, not insane, and that I'd love to have dinner with him sometime…but I'm pretty sure he would have escorted me out of town with flashing lights and accompanying sirens.

Was that the reception I would get upon being truthful?

Would my admission now solve the murder my grandmother was implicated in fifty-three years ago? Did her secret have anything to do with Jacob Blackleach?

If ever I believed in intuition, it was now.

*Yes* reverberated in my head after every single question, though it wasn't Leo responding. That had definitely been my subconscious. But telling the truth would have a cost I wasn't so sure I was ready to pay at the moment.

Leo won this battle…for now.

"Yes," I replied with a victorious smile, picking up my phone and waving it in the air. "Can you believe my phone was sitting here the entire time?"

Larry's gaze went from my hand to the counter numerous times, his light brown brows dipping down in a massive frown. It was a good thing he had light-colored eyebrows. Anything darker would have looked a bit off with the bald style he was trying to pull off.

"I could have sworn…"

"Raven, what is this?"

Thankfully, Liam cut off Larry's curiosity as to how my phone had ended up beside the cash register when we'd already looked in that area.

Liam.

Leo.

Larry.

There was an obvious theme going on with these new people in my life, but I would have to put that coincidence on the back burner. Speaking of burners, I had way too many fires burning. I wasn't sure which one to put out first.

I also should have known not to count my blessings, especially with the way my week had been going. Liam was looking in the small basket I'd brought out front from the back room. I'd wanted to see who else in this town had standing orders, and who might want something from the list of names in the ledger. My intention had been to put the basket back in the storage room, but I'd forgotten after getting so caught up talking to Leo about Nan's witchcraft.

Witchcraft.

I was still repeating the word over and over in my head, thinking that any moment I would wake up in my one bedroom apartment, having had the most vivid dream.

Unfortunately, that didn't happen.

Liam decided to light another fire, though. This time, he'd soaked the ground with gasoline before striking a match.

"How could you not have told me that Jacob Blackleach was one of your grandmother's clients?"

# Chapter Nine

"LEO, HOW COULD you not remember that Jacob Black-leach was one of Nan's clients?"

*You're the one who had the paper bags right in front of you. The names were scrawled across the front of each order, so don't blame me because you missed it. I might be suffering from short term memory loss, but you're the one who needs glasses.*

I was at a loss. I no longer had Nan's ledger to look through. Liam had confiscated the tiny treasure for the state police, leaving me with little to go on in solving Jacob Blackleach's murder. The little bit of control I had over this situation had been taken out of my hands, and there wasn't a thing I could do about it.

Well, that wasn't entirely true.

I could vent to the odd-looking furball lounging on the coffee table in front of me as if he didn't have a care in the world. He even had the audacity to continuously flick his tail. No, it wouldn't do me any good to yell at a cat who could appear and disappear at will. Instead, I turned my attention on Ted, who looked as if he wanted to be anywhere but here.

"You know that all of this could have been avoided had the little Persian king himself told me this tiny bit of news. Did you know Jacob Blackleach was a client?"

"Yes."

I closed my eyes and prayed for more patience, having already accepted that Ted's short replies were going to be the death of me. Speaking of death…

"Ted, was he more than a client? Why would Jacob pretend to be Larry Butterball?"

*Oh, that's easy.*

Leo squinted his eyes as if he were debating to share this enlightenment, but I took a step forward to show him that I was done playing around. I wasn't sure I could take any more surprises with all this witchcraft talk.

*Jacob wanted Rosemary's spells. He needed them.*

"What did Mr. Leo say?"

I hastily did a double take, believing I'd heard Ted wrong. I quickly realized that Ted couldn't hear a word Leo said.

It appeared only I had that pleasure.

"Leo said that Jacob wanted Nan's spells. Something about needing them," I translated, grateful that I didn't have to hide my conversations with a cat like I had to do earlier today in front of Liam and Larry. That could get downright exhausting. I'd never been good at keeping secrets, so my immediate future was looking pretty lonely. "Wait. Nan has a spell book, too? Not just for recipes?"

*Yes.*

"Jacob *was* your grandmother's client, but he was also more than that." Ted frowned at Leo, but it wasn't because the cat hadn't been right in his assumption of Jacob Blackleach. It had more to do with Leo only giving me the bare minimum of information. "Mr. Leo, tell the whole truth."

*Very well.*

Leo flicked his tail a little harder on the wooden surface of the coffee table to show his displeasure. Why did he want to make things so difficult for me? I was beginning to get a complex over a cat that preferred his own death over my company. What had I done to deserve this kind of karma in my life?

*It's relatively simple. You see, Jacob was a wizard, having come from a long lineage of magic from the Blackleach clan. His knowledge of certain powers was weak in comparison to your family's mastery of the eight spheres of magic, and he wanted your grandmother's spells for conjuration and invocation. Technically, he coveted a special incantation that would allow him to summon the spirits of his dead ancestors.*

"That doesn't sound like a good idea," I said, only to then repeat everything Leo had divulged so that Ted was kept dialed into the conversation. It was wearing on me, but I liked having Ted in my corner. "Did Nan say yes?"

*Of course not. Jacob then practically begged Rosemary to create a spell that would locate a long lost relative. You see, the power of three is real. Jacob was hoping to reunite with his older brother, who had been shunned from his family for falling in love with a member of the Carsington coven. Now that was a powerful family who somehow managed to stay together after the witch trials of 1651.*

"Leo, why didn't you tell me all this earlier? This explains why Jacob pretended to be Larry Butterball. Jacob had to have believed that either my mother or I have access to that particular spell book he'd been seeking this entire time." I couldn't believe Leo had been holding onto this important information. Liam needed to know at least some of this, because it spoke to Jacob's motivation. Ultimately, all of this could lead to an arrest. I couldn't imagine living Nan's secret life where I had to keep my entire existence hidden from the good residents of this town. Cora Barnes suddenly sprang to mind. Okay, so not all the residents in Paramour Bay were nice. "Ted, I need to drive back into town."

*Do I have to hide your keys the way I did your phone?*

Leo stood on all four paws and stretched his back as if he was just starting out his day. He even yawned for effect, but his casual attitude didn't match the threat in his tone. He was totally serious.

*You cannot tell Heidi that you are a witch, just as you cannot share with the sheriff that Jacob Blackleach was a wizard. Nor can you reveal that his family was involved with magic. Revealing that you are a witch will only lead to a recipe that will spell disaster. None of the magical families are able to reveal their true existence. Ordinary people can be dangerous, especially those envious of your differences. The covens have a standing agreement to keep each other's secrets and to not reveal the existence of the true nature of magic to the fearful public.*

I'm pretty sure that Leo snickered at the pun he'd just formed, but I was over his sarcastic replies.

I didn't even bother to translate Leo's sentiments to Ted, who wasn't even paying attention to my one-sided conversation with Leo anymore. The gentle giant was looking off into space as if he was a lovestruck teenager longing for his smart phone. I began to wonder if he didn't have a crush on Mindy Walsh, who he had visited at the boutique today. That would be rather odd, considering I thought he was a...

I couldn't even finish that thought, because I already had enough stress in my life over the supernatural elements circling over my head. What I needed to do right this minute was solve this murder so that I was no longer standing in Sheriff Liam's path waiting for the inevitable feel of cold steel on my wrists.

*Who are you fooling?* Leo asked, hopping off the coffee table only to take up residence on the windowsill. *I saw the way you looked at that young sheriff today.*

"You saw no such thing." I denied his assertion, and rather vehemently, too. I refused to get into an argument with a cat over a man I found somewhat attractive. There were some lines that I couldn't bring myself to cross, and one of them was discussing my love life with an ordinary housecat with a superiority complex who was currently in the shape of a hairball that looked like it had been run over by a truck.

*Take that back.*

Leo hissed my way, but his snaggled tooth dimmed his intent.

*I'm not ordinary.*

Once again, I wasn't going to argue with Nan's cat. I needed a plan, because Leo was actually right, in a manner of speaking. I didn't want anyone else realizing I was a witch, when I wasn't sure that was what I was to begin with. Wouldn't I feel different somehow? Wouldn't my body sense that I harnessed some type of natural power? The capability should manifest itself somehow.

Where were my powers?

Capturing the individual responsible for Jacob Blackleach's murder needed to be my first priority, so that I could then concentrate on learning everything I could about my family's history and the lineage of our coven.

Of course, that meant talking with my mother and getting her to tell me the simple truth, but that couldn't happen until this weekend at the earliest—meaning I had five days to figure out the identity of the killer and let the sheriff arrest him or her.

*You are not Daphne, Ted is not Fred, and I am certainly not Scooby Doo.*

Leo settled in on the windowpane and stared out into the darkness as if he were offended to be compared to a dog, but he'd been the one who had made the comparison. He could only be mad at himself for the inference.

*Let the bumbling sheriff do his own job, while you do yours— which is learning to harness your powers properly. You know, the ones you seem to think you don't have. The boxes of notes your grandmother left for you are upstairs in the loft underneath your bed.*

"The sheriff would be more than capable of finding out who killed Jacob Blackleach if he knew the real truth," I said in my defense of Liam. It wasn't fair that he got a bad rap for not knowing the facts about what was really happening in his town. Besides, he hadn't even been born during the first murder my Nan was involved in fifty-three years ago. "Leo, you told me that you saw the individual who murdered Jacob Blackleach. You need to remember who it was so that I can go to the sheriff with some kind of story. I'll come up with some plausible excuse other than witchcraft as to why Jacob was here to be murdered in the first place."

*I don't remember.*

"But you saw it happen," I argued, not willing to let this go. I focused on Ted, who had gone back to staring off into space. We were so close to figuring out who killed Jacob, and yet I was stuck with these two clowns. "Ted, did you hear anything while you were inside the boutique? Did Mindy mention the murder or who she thought could be responsible? Did she see any strangers walking around town?"

"Miss Mindy would never talk out of turn. She is a lady."

"I didn't say she…"

I let my words trail off as a headache began to form behind my temples. Ted was taking things way too literally for me to deal with him right now. I purposefully moved to the couch and sat down on the overstuffed cushion, closing my eyes and taking a deep breath the way Heidi had taught me during the one yoga class we attended last year as a free introductory lesson. I continued to monitor my breathing and clear my mind as I brought my boots up underneath my skirt, making myself more comfortable on my perch.

"Cora Barnes asked Miss Mindy to sell the boutique today."

I popped open my right eye, peering at Ted to see if he understood how revealing that small bit of truth had been. I wasn't sure he was even capable of lying, but this bit of news meant Cora and Desmond were more than serious about expanding the malt shop.

Ted's sunken cheeks somehow became hollower as he tilted head to the side and stared back at me, almost as if he'd never seen someone in the meditation position. Maybe he hadn't. Nan hadn't been one to contemplate yoga when she could be getting her nails painted at the salon.

"Cora asked Mindy this today?" I asked, just to confirm what I'd heard. I lowered my lashes and took another deep breath. It was in that exact moment that I figured out how I could take advantage of Ted and Leo's knowledge. I quickly lowered my black boots from the couch and leaned forward before searching through coffee table drawers for a notepad and pen. "And was Mindy one of Nan's clients?"

"Oh, no," Ted said emphatically, shaking his head continuously until Leo intervened with a meow. "Mr. Leo, I don't know what you're saying to Miss Raven, but Miss Mindy is a good woman of faith."

I really wanted to go down that interesting path, wondering if Ted truly believed that Nan wasn't a good person because she'd used witchcraft in a wrong manner. But that little peccadillo wouldn't solve this murder, so I would have to save that topic for another day.

What I needed right now was a list of names and to find someone who could tell me if anyone they knew in Paramour Bay was capable of murder. Well, besides Liam. I almost stopped looking for that notepad when it dawned on me that maybe one of the Carsingtons had murdered Jacob because of some old family feud. I'm glad I didn't.

"Leo, what exactly is this?" I asked, spinning toward the window while holding up what I firmly believed to be the same ledger as the one Liam had taken into evidence for the state police. Oh, no, he didn't. I continued to deny what was in my grasp, needing confirmation. "What did you do?"

*I did what had to be done. There is a pact to be upheld.*

Leo's snaggled tooth was showing a little more than usual. Was he sneering at me?

*When you're done playing amateur detective, let me know, and then we'll begin your training. Otherwise, you can drag Ted's carcass around town while you do the sheriff's job for him.*

And just like that, Leo was gone.

Vanished.

I mean, it was like he never existed.

"You shouldn't yell at Mr. Leo in his fragile state." Ted sighed as if he were talking with to a toddler. I was beginning to wonder how Nan had dealt with these two on a daily basis. "You'll find that Miss Mindy's name is not in that ledger."

I didn't reply, but instead sat back down on the couch and opened the leather-bound book. The ledger not only contained a list of clients and what their reasons were for seeking out Nan's help, but it also served as a protracted calendar of sorts. Beside each name were dates and times, seemingly a rather regular schedule at that.

It was quite similar to the calendar of tea orders I'd found in one of the drawers at the shop.

This type of organizational skills made it somewhat easier, yet difficult, to find what I was looking for in the midst of names. What I was searching for was motive, means, and opportunity. And I truly hoped none of those things included revealing my family's secrets.

And there it was staring right back at me as if the letters had been highlighted in yellow—evidence that Cora Barnes was supposed to have been in the shop at the time Jacob Blackleach was murdered.

"Ted, I found it! I found it," I exclaimed, scrambling to my feet before heading to the door. I snatched my purse off the side table, along with my keys, and opened the door. "I'm going to find Liam and tell him who the killer is, all without revealing my newfound heritage. Ted, I'm a genius!"

# Chapter Ten

OKAY, SO I wasn't exactly a genius.

The night I went to find Liam to tell him about my brilliant deduction, he'd been at the local pub. In all honesty, I didn't even know Paramour Bay had a pub of any sort. The building wasn't even located on River Bay itself, but instead sat off of Water Way in a charming English-style dart bar. They had several local brews on tap and was now officially my favorite microbrewery.

I'd run into Eileen as I was walking back to my car from the police station. She'd been leaving a small theater that played movies not exactly on their first run. You know the kind, the ones that had been released three months ago in places like New York City. I highly doubt that the place held fifty couples when it was full, but then again, I'd never been inside. That small treat would have to wait for a time when I wasn't living my own classic horror movie.

*You know, you've been poring over those notes for days. We need to begin your training.*

"Leo, look at this as preparation for that training. Every bit of family insight will help me in that endeavor, which I'm still not sure what to expect from your so-called *training*. Besides, we still have no idea where Nan hid her spell book."

*I know where it is.*

My head whipped up from the journal I was reading regarding my great-great-great grandmother's life, though there was no mention of witchcraft. Had Leo finally pulled through on something of importance? The fact that his green eyes were narrowed told me otherwise.

*I had it there for a second. Oops, now it's gone.*

It took all my might not to lay my forehead down on the counter with a feeling of complete defeat. A lot had happened over the past three days, yet nothing of significance. Other than realizing Nan had left me a faulty set of instructions in Leo.

Getting back to the night I'd thought of myself as a bona fide genius, it turns out that Cora Barnes had been hosting a lunch for the local ladies' auxiliary at the public library in one of their back rooms. She'd decided to forgo picking up her order, seeing as I'd yet to open the store officially.

At least, that was her excuse.

I'm still not sure I believed her statement to the police.

I couldn't allow my disappointment to be noticeable, especially since Liam had been very appreciative that I'd been attempting to think outside the box when it came to Jacob's murder. I ended up telling him a little white lie about there being a sticky note underneath the cash register about what time Cora had been supposed to pick up her order at the shop. He hadn't been told yet by the state police detective that the ledger had gone missing, so I'd had to fudge a bit on how I'd been made aware of that information.

I'd even gone so far as to suggest that maybe Cora had thought I'd already be open for business, not expecting to run into a conman who had been impersonating Larry Butterball. I even tossed out the theory that Jacob's murder could have been in self-defense if she'd chanced upon him while he was robbing the shop. Looking back, I'd been a chatterbox and couldn't stop the various scenarios about last Sunday from escaping my lips.

It was clear to see that Liam wasn't buying every little assumption I had told him, either, but I *had* seen a small glimmer of interest in his brown gaze. He was keener than Leo had given him credit for, and I had a hunch Liam observed a lot more than anyone initially realized.

*Why are you focusing so much on Cora Barnes?*

"Because that's who I believe killed Jacob Blackleach," I said, sitting back on the high-top stool behind the cash register of the shop. "Cora had opportunity. I just can't prove it. I'm not so sure the murder had anything to do with this so-called witchcraft. I think she panicked, and Desmond helped her cover it up, because she was surprised by Jacob's presence. Or maybe Desmond is the killer. You know, I hadn't thought of that. Maybe he was caught in a fit of jealousy."

*You watched a lot of television as a child, didn't you?*

I ignored Leo and the fact that his left eye became even larger in his speculation. I'd been up since five o'clock this morning preparing for the grand opening of *Tea, Leaves, & Eves*. My nerves were on edge due to my limited knowledge of…well…basically everything to do with the beverage.

*I said I'd help with the customers, so relax.*

Leo was currently lounging in the display window, showing his better side to the public. I was a bit surprised at that, considering he only ever let me or Ted see his physical form. With that said, only one person had walked past since I'd come into the shop early, and that was a young woman around my age with chestnut colored hair. I was banking on her being Mindy Walsh, but I would have to introduce myself later.

A bit of panic had set in that I was trusting a cat with short term memory loss to help me sell tea products to customers who knew more about the soothing beverage than I did.

The truth was beginning to set in.

*Do you feel any differently today?*

"That's the fourth time you asked me in the past hour." I glanced down at my half-empty cup of English Breakfast tea with distaste, wishing more now than ever that it was a vanilla latte with skim milk, two shots of espresso, and no foam. Maybe I could sneak a Keurig machine in the back. "Does feeling a bit more irritated than usual count?"

*That's your mother's doing. Not mine.*

Leo stretched out his back legs when the sun's rays moved a bit to the right, becoming more comfortable and seemingly believing his own pronouncement.

*I still don't understand why you didn't tell Regina about me or the fact that you know about your family history.*

"Because that's not the type of conversation one has over the phone, especially with my own mother."

*You were going to tell Heidi.*

"That's entirely different," I argued, hoping that no one saw me carrying on a conversation with a cat who looked a bit worse for wear. Of course, that was better than anyone believing I was talking to myself. I suppose I should be grateful that Leo was displayed in the window for all to see. I could always say he got stuck in a trash compactor and had somehow miraculously survived. "And I can pretty much guarantee that Heidi will be accompanying my mother here on Friday, because I've been ignoring her latest texts."

*Then don't ignore her texts.*

"And end up lying to her?" I asked incredulously, slamming the book I was reading closed just as the alarm on my phone chimed to remind me it was nine o'clock in the morning. It was time to flip the open sign on the front door and take *Tea, Leaves, & Eves'* first customer. "No one lies to Heidi and survives. That would only make things worse. I still have two days to figure things out."

I hopped off the stool and reluctantly walked to the door as I recalled my meeting with Larry on Monday morning. It had gone better than expected, and every single detail that Jacob Blackleach had told me regarding Nan's estate had been true. It was the reason I'd been poring over the boxes of family information my grandmother had left me, but so far, there had been nothing in those records to indicate that Leo was telling the truth about any history of witchcraft.

*You're not looking in the right boxes.*

"Then tell me which ones are the right ones, Leo. Better yet, tell me where that darn spell book is," I practically pleaded, finally finding the courage to flip the sign. I really needed something stronger than tea if I was going to make it through the day. "Maybe it's a good thing I haven't brought this up to my mother, because there's still a slight chance I've gone absolutely bonkers since my arrival."

*Do you feel any different?*

Are you wondering why Leo keeps asking me that?

Well, it's because today is my birthday. My thirtieth birthday, and yet the sun still rose and the clock kept ticking.

The expected day I'm supposed to obtain my unearthly powers.

"No, Leo, I don't feel the slightest bit different."

The bell chimed above the door before I had even made it back to the counter.

My heart fluttered.

My first customer had just arrived.

Well, if you discount Pearl, Elsie, and Wilma. Those had been clients of Nan's side business. And I totally understand why she would sell potions and hex bags to the residents of Paramour Bay. The majority of the orders I'd read up in the ledger had to do with health ailments, though one or two had to do with her surreal concoction of love remedies. I didn't necessarily agree with those types of magical blends, but that was something I could sort out at another time.

"Good morning," a cheerful voice rang out, telling me that this happy being had ingested coffee at some point before leaving her home. It made me wonder why she was in a tea shop. "You must be Raven. Flo came by yesterday and couldn't say enough good things about you. And I'm so sorry about your first day here. It must have been shocking. I can't imagine finding someone dead five minutes after arriving in town. I'm Candy Butler, by the way. I own the beauty salon down the road, between Brook Cove and Lake Drive. I hope you get a chance to stop by soon."

"Hi, Candy," I replied with a matching smile. Her happiness was infectious. "It's nice to meet you."

*What is that color on her head?*

Okay. In Leo's defense, the reddish orange dye in Candy's hair reminded me of a Jolly Rancher. Or maybe a jellybean. It was Halloween, after all. I'm not sure, but the color of her hair had nothing to do with the positive vibes coming off this woman's aura.

*And there it is.*

I refrained from jumping up and down in exhilaration at the fact that Leo had finally been proven right.

Vibes?

Aura?

I'd never in a million years ever paid attention to anyone's aura before in my life, but this was a woman I could become friends with during my time in Paramour Bay.

"Do you know if your grandmother has received the pumpkin spice flavored black tea leaves in her last shipment? It's my absolute favorite, especially this time of the year and all."

My irritable mood from earlier dissipated into a cloud of mist and was immediately replaced with euphoria. Not only had I seen the log of the last shipment, I'd even put the loose tea leaves in the appropriate containers.

On top of that?

I'd even studied the label and would be able to discuss the properties of the tea.

This day was going to be the best one yet!

"The shipment did come in, and I have it right here." I proceeded happily across the shop until I'd reached the appropriate shelf. Nan had been smart to put the shelves within reach. "Would you like four, eight, or sixteen ounces? Just a small reminder, the caffeine content of this leaf is a medium level, whereas the antioxidant levels are exceptionally high."

"Sixteen ounces, please," Candy replied, though her voice was no longer coming from the middle of the store. I turned to find her walking a bit closer to Leo, who was staring at her with his somewhat larger left eye. "Oh, you poor thing. Is he a rescue from some horrible accident?"

*Do something before I bite her.*

"You might say that. Believe it or not, Leo found me."

"You know, he looks an awful lot like Rosemary's old cat. I'm assuming Ted has been taking care of Benny, but did something happen to—"

"Benny? Ted?"

*Not one word, Raven. Not one.*

Two things immediately sprang to my mind, the most vital being the fact that Candy spoke about Ted as if he were indeed a typical resident of Paramour Bay. Did no one find it rather odd that an overly large-sized man who'd most likely never visited a dentist and was constantly cold to the touch lived in a shed on the back of my grandmother's property?

*You know, I'm remembering something from that morning. Candy was…*

I almost dropped the glass container of tea leaves as I swung back around, my heart stuttering over the chance that Leo had finally gotten his memory back of the events that happened with Jacob.

*Nope. Wrong day. Carry on.*

It was a good thing these glass containers were so thick, because my knuckles had turned white in my attempt to control my irritation at Leo and his blurting fits.

"Yes, Benny. He wasn't the nicest of cats, but he'd been perfectly healthy unlike this…well, this poor thing."

*That's it. I've had enough.*

"Candy, do you work on Saturday?" I managed to get the hairstylist to focus on me before Leo's fang and a half ended up in the back of her hand. "I was thinking I could come in and have a small trim. Oh, and Leo is a rescue I brought with me from New York. Ted must have Benny, and I'm sure the two of them are like two peas in a pod."

I found it easier to stick closer to the truth, because I figured it was only a matter of time before I messed this whole thing up. Then again, the two peas in a pod analogy was quite a stretch for me.

"I do work Saturdays," Candy exclaimed excitedly, spinning around to focus on me just as I'd hoped she would. I certainly didn't expect her to rush over and invade my personal space while touching my hair, but her enthusiasm for a new client came through by leaps and bounds. "The color of your hair is amazing, just like Rosemary's tresses. I always said that her hair shimmered with a rich purple if the light caught it just so, and darn if yours doesn't do the very same."

We ended up talking more about hairstyles than we did the properties of the tea leaves I was selling her, but I was okay with that topic given the circumstances. It didn't take long for me to get her order ready, having practiced with the amazing machine herb weighing and packaging machine that must have cost my grandmother a fortune.

I can even admit to inhaling deeply quite a few times as I poured the tea leaves in the top opening of the appliance. The aroma was heavenly, and even reminded me of the pumpkin spiced coffee that I loved during the fall season from my once favorite coffee shop back in New York.

Of course, after ringing up the price of the tea leaves at twelve dollars and ninety-nine cents, I figured the machine was well worth the investment. And the added bonus? I was going to try this tea the moment Candy left the shop.

"Here comes Dee Fairuza. I just love that woman. Her hair is divine."

Sure enough, another customer opened the door to the tea shop and entered with a fresh breeze. There was something flowery about this woman's aura. I know, that didn't make a lick of sense, but there it was, plain as day.

Dee had the most beautiful colored bronze skin that reminded me of some exotic island, but I couldn't pinpoint her ethnicity. It didn't matter. She'd brought in happiness through the door, as well.

*Don't go all hippie on me.*

I ignored Leo's little jab, but that was easier than I thought it would be after Candy steered the conversation toward the murder. I wasn't sure how to explain that moment, other than similar to when the flame on a match was blown out with one fast exhale.

"I heard Larry contacted Abbie," Candy mentioned to Dee, leaning against my counter as if it were the water cooler at the office. "She was pretty upset that he thought that she had anything to do with that man who impersonated Larry. Oh, I'm sorry. Where are my manners? Dee, this is Raven. Raven, Dee Fairuzo."

"It's nice to meet you, Raven. Could I have eight ounces of the apple spice flavored black tea? I'm almost out, and it's my usual morning blend." Dee then focused dark brown eyes on Candy, but I didn't take offense. I wanted to hear what Dee had to say about Abbie Butterball just as much as Candy did, so I walked across the store to where the flavored tea leaves were located while hanging onto every word uttered behind my back. "Abbie about had a cow, believing that Larry was accusing her of setting him up somehow. You know how ugly their divorce got, but that was a new low for Larry to accuse her of such machinations."

"Did he actually accuse her of hiring Jacob Blackleach? You know, that good-looking detective came into the shop waving about that picture of the dead guy. I'd never seen him before, but he didn't resemble Abbie in the slightest."

"And that's exactly what Abbie told Larry when he called her the other day." Dee reached into her purse and pulled out her wallet after I'd weighed and packaged her tea leaves. I cheated a bit and looked in the book next to the cash register to read about the caffeine content and the antioxidant levels. I was a bit relieved when she didn't ask anything about it. "You've met Larry, right?"

*This is a trap.*

I shot Leo a sideways glance. Did he really believe I was that naïve?

*Do you want me to answer that?*

"Yes," I responded to Dee after taking the ten-dollar bill from her hand. I quickly counted out her change after making a mental note to bring in a credit card machine. It was high time this tea shop upgraded and caught up with technology. "I met him on Sunday. I was so sorry that his vacation was cut short, but Jacob Blackleach did try to take over his identity. It was probably a good thing he came back to sort things out."

"He shouldn't be dragging Abbie into his problems, though," Dee said with a bit of a huff, her loyalty to Abbie shining through like sunlight glistening off a diamond. This petite exotic woman reminded me so very much of Heidi. "She's been through quite enough already."

"Is Hannah trick or treating tonight?" Candy asked, pulling her cell phone out of her purse and checking the time. It seemed like no one wore a watch anymore. Everyone had a phone with every bit of information one could ever want on it. I figured the hair salon opened at ten o'clock, so she still had time. "I was thinking of allowing Jade to go one more year, seeing as she will turn twelve next month."

Now that the conversation had steered away from Jacob Blackleach, I went about cleaning up the loose debris around the machine and putting everything back in place. At least these women hadn't treated me like some type of criminal, but then again, they seemed to connect Jacob to Larry due to the role reversal. That wasn't quite fair of them.

*And let's leave it at that. The last thing we need is for them to think there's something odd with you.*

"There's nothing odd with..." I began to protest, turning to find both women staring at me with amazement. I managed to swallow my embarrassment, and even better yet, cover my tracks in order to make them believe I'd joined in on the conversation. "Trick or treating at age eleven. It's my thirtieth birthday today, and I used to celebrate by dressing up and seeing how much candy I could haul in each Halloween night."

A chorus of *Happy birthdays* from the two women were announced before turning the conversation back to what age was appropriate to stop dressing up in costumes and joining in the festivities of trick or treating. This went on for another two minutes or so before something came to me that I realized could be answered with a simple response.

"Candy, do you know if anyone in town *did* recognize Jacob Blackleach?" If there was one person in Paramour Bay who would have all the town's gossip, it would definitely be the hairstylist. "You mentioned that Detective Swanson came by with a picture, so I was wondering if he had any luck finding out any information that could help his case."

Before Candy could answer, the bell above the door chimed once more.

*It's like Grand Central Station in here.*

I kept forgetting about Leo until he'd offer his two cents, which I could well afford not to have today. I was making plenty of sales, and didn't need his spare change.

"Ladies."

Lo and behold, it was Sheriff Liam Drake.

His smile, which he didn't do often enough, was almost enough to make me forget about the coffee he held in his hand that had no doubt come from Trixie's Diner. I would have returned his greeting had he not ruined my morning.

"Raven, I thought I'd best be the first one to tell you that I just gave your mother a parking ticket."

# Chapter Eleven

"YOU DID NO such thing," I disputed adamantly, refusing to believe that my mother had driven into Paramour Bay two days early without so much as letting me know she was coming. Heck, I wasn't even sure she'd show up on Friday. It took me less than three seconds to bypass Liam and peer out the glass door. "It's not nice to joke about family visiting me from out of the blue, especially on my birthday."

I made it seem that it meant the world to me that my mother would come to town, not wanting anyone here to know that the very thought of the upcoming confrontation gave me an ulcer. It was a relief not to see my mother's vehicle parked out front.

*Look the other way.*

I took Leo's advice, and my stomach plummeted to my feet.

"She must have arrived early for your big day," Candy replied with a clap of her hands. I wish I had her exuberance, but it was all I could do to hold the tea I drank earlier from coming back up my throat. "You know, I think I remember your mother. Don't get me wrong, I couldn't have been more than five years old or so at the time. But I recall seeing her walk by the playground over on Lake Drive every day after school."

It didn't escape my notice that Candy didn't say whether or not my mother had been a nice person back then. Honestly, I didn't want to talk about my mom with any of them. I wanted everyone to leave so that I could confront what was sure to be the ultimate battle of wills.

"I really need to head on out," Dee said regrettably, although unknowingly giving me a bit of hope that no one would be around to witness the bloodshed. "I need to walk over to Mindy's shop to find the last accessory for Hannah's outfit tonight. Raven, thanks for the blend."

"You're quite welcome." My words came out more as a mumble as I stared at my mother's vehicle, wondering what she was waiting for before opening her door. What was she doing inside her car? "You have a nice day, and I'm sure I'll see you and Hannah this evening."

"I should be going, too," Candy said with reluctance, obviously having wanted to stay and meet the infamous Regina Marigold—the woman who'd been notoriously cut out of Rosemary's will. That would definitely have made good fodder for her clients today. It wasn't until I moved out of the way for Candy to exit that she finally answered my previous question. "And yes, someone did recognize Jacob Blackleach. Flo said she'd seen him in the diner a time or two, though no one else could remember his face for some reason."

How could no one else but Flo remember Jacob Blackleach? The diner maintained numerous regulars who ate there on a daily basis for every meal, as well as the staff the diner employed. Could he have used some spell to make the patrons forget his passing? Had his magic not worked on Flo because she'd been his waitress and exposed to his presence more than the others?

Jacob was a wizard, but he'd been weak from what Leo had said.

I waited for Leo to confirm my suspicion, but all I received was silence. A quick glance toward the window display told me he'd abandoned me in my time of need.

"Here."

The tender way Liam addressed me was enough to drag my gaze off the empty windowsill Leo had occupied. Liam was holding out his cup of coffee, but it finally sunk in that it wasn't his.

He'd brought me my own coffee.

The bonus points this got him overrode my need to know why he'd given my mother a parking ticket. He could give her all the tickets he wanted. He'd just granted me my birthday wish.

My eyes drifted up to his, and it took all of my will not to throw my arms around his neck.

"Happy birthday, Raven." The corner of Liam's lip lifted in a half-grin. "Just make sure you hide it behind the cash register. Spotting a coffee cup in a tea shop probably isn't good for your business."

With a wink, Liam exited the shop.

*Okay, I take it back. He might be a keeper, after all.*

Of course, Leo would choose to make an entrance now. He couldn't just leave me to have one second of happiness, could he?

I would have told Leo to tie his whiskers in a knot, but I was too busy sucking down the most delicious cup of coffee I'd ever tasted in my life. Granted, it could have used a bit more sugar, but I wasn't going to come off ungrateful after such an amazing gift.

Unfortunately, there was no amount of caffeine in the world that could help me deal with the upcoming confrontation.

Why hadn't Heidi given me a heads up?

*I'm sure she did.*

Leo continued to swish his bent tail as he made his way toward the back room.

*But you left your phone at home. Remember? And before you blame me, you left it on the coffee table when you were looking for the spell book.*

"You mean the spell book that you can't remember the location of?" I quickly followed Leo toward the back, knowing I only had a few moments to spare. "I'm being serious here, Leo. If I need to know something about Nan or of our family's lineage from that witchcrafty stuff, then tell me now. I need to be prepared before my mother walks through that door."

*Witchcrafty stuff?*

I'm relatively sure Leo's left eye rolled at my language.

*You're a witch, Raven, that much is certain. By midnight, you will be one with the all-mother earth. There is nothing your birth mother can do now to change your future.*

And just like that…Leo was gone.

Poof.

Vanished.

Again.

It was beyond frustrating, but nowhere near as maddening as the fact that my mother was about to walk through the door.

Sure enough, the gold bell chimed, leaving me little choice but to take a deep breath and turn around to face the incoming nor' westerly.

Okay, Regina Lattice Marigold was more like a tornado than a winter storm.

We stared at one another without saying a word, each of us sizing up one another.

I should preface this next scene with the fact that I do love my mother very much. She's always put me first and made sure I didn't want for anything as a child. She'd been strict yet fair. I wasn't always the easiest young girl to get along with, having a wild streak a country mile wide that I needed to paint with vivid colors like a rainbow. She'd let me spread my wings while somehow keeping me close and safe.

But to find out that she'd kept from me such life-altering knowledge about our family had been wrong, and her walking into my tea shop and demanding I return to the city was unacceptable.

I didn't have to ask why she was here, because as I said, that much was obvious—she wanted me back in New York City and as far away from Paramour Bay as she could get me.

Only that wasn't going to happen now that I knew the truth.

"You *know*," my mother accused me as she rested a hand against her forehead in disbelief. She'd always been a little dramatic, but that was understandable, considering how she'd been raised. But darn if her answer didn't remind me of Leo, who was constantly in my head. "You know about the family. Oh, dear. I think I'm going to be sick."

My mother's green eyes widened in what I could only describe as dread. Her black hair was pulled back at the nape of her neck, which was the way she usually styled her hair. She always claimed that she didn't like the weight of her hair on her shoulders, but she could never bring herself to cut the beautiful jet-black tresses. And yet she'd cut Nan out of our lives, or vice versa.

Did it really matter anymore?

"I would have known a long time ago if you'd just been honest with me, Mom." No one else was in the shop but us, yet I still found it hard to verbalize my newfound knowledge. "Nan was a witch. You were a witch. *Are* a witch. And now I'm a witch, yet you kept that from me. How could you do that?"

"To protect you." Regina audibly sighed as she began to

slowly scan the shop. Was she looking for Leo? No, she had to be searching for something else. She couldn't even know the odd familiar was still alive, albeit somewhat damaged. "And I would do it all over again. Raven, I never wanted you to live that life. You don't understand the responsibilities that come with this kind of curse."

"Gift," I corrected, having seen Otis walking down the sidewalk with his wife yesterday. He hadn't been in pain, because his arthritis was being kept to a minimum, thanks to Nan's herbal potion. Then there was Larry's athlete's foot. I mean, really. Who wanted to walk around with itching toes all day? "Nan helped people, Mom. She used her powers for good, and we could do the same. It wasn't fair of you to keep this from me. It's my birthright."

"I intentionally walked away from this life a very long time ago, Raven Lattice." Regina shook her head as she walked over to the cash register. She stored her purse underneath the counter as if she'd done it numerous times in the past. "And that's exactly what you're going to do. Whatever papers my mother left you to tell you about our family history, you need to burn them tonight. I'll help you close up the shop, then we can head to the house to get your belongings. We'll return to the city as if none of this ever happened."

I couldn't believe what I was hearing, let alone accept that she was treating me as if I were two years old. I'd told Heidi on the day we arrived in town that I needed to stand on my own two feet. It was about time I owned up to my declaration.

"Mother, I didn't learn about our gift from a box of papers, though I will admit that there are some very entertaining family tales in those letters." I wasn't lying when I said that, either. I'd come to find out that not one woman in my family who had been born with their powers had ever married. Wasn't that odd? I wanted to know more. My appetite for my family's history was insatiable, but I would have to continue my search on that another day. "Nan used a necromancy spell on her familiar to stay behind and teach me the ways of our family. Now before you say anything, I understand fully well that she shouldn't have dabbled in dark magic. But she didn't feel she had a choice, because you were the one to cut her out of your life. You did that, right?"

It was more than apparent that my mom wanted to address several issues with the things I'd just mentioned, but she wasn't sure where to start.

I chose for her.

"I'm right, aren't I?" I didn't need her to answer, because something inherent told me that I'd speculated correctly. I could get used to this witch intuition. Crossing the room, I stood across the counter from her so I could see her reaction. I'd said it didn't matter who was responsible for the family rift, but I was wrong. "I didn't show signs of my power, so Nan left us alone after I'd turned eighteen. But it wasn't by her choice. It was obviously yours."

"You don't understand, Raven. She would have found a way to drag you into this life, which is not what I wanted for you. We are cursed with these powers. How can you not see that? As for Benny? Please tell me that she didn't use a spell so dark and evil as to keep her familiar alive that—"

The bell chimed over the front door, causing me to immediately shove the disposable coffee cup that was still in my hand into hers. I then turned around with a smile on my face, refusing to have the residents of Paramour Bay churn the gossip mill with the Marigold name. The last thing we needed was to have more attention on us than there was already due to Jacob Blackleach's murder.

"I thought that was you, Regina. And drinking coffee, no less. It's no wonder that you and your mother weren't on speaking terms."

My smile slipped at the sight of Cora Barnes. I tried my best to keep it in place, but that was next to impossible. There was something sinister about this woman's presence…adversarial in nature. It didn't help that her blonde hair was pulled back so severely that there didn't seem to be a wrinkle left underneath all that makeup. That could not have been an easy feat considering that she had to be in her mid-fifties.

Mid-fifties.

The connection hit me at the exact moment my mother confirmed my intuition—you know, the one I was grateful for around an hour ago.

"Cora, you haven't changed a bit."

"It's been…what? Almost thirty years?" Cora's smile didn't meet her eyes, which were one hundred percent focused on my mother. I was beginning to understand how Ted felt during those times I had conversations with Leo. "I'd honestly expected it to be longer. You have my condolences."

It was as if I could literally hear the electricity spark from each and every correlation matching up that I'd arrived to in my mind. Thirty years. It was my thirtieth birthday. And the two women were around the same age, so it was no wonder they knew each other from their younger days.

"You can keep your condolences, Cora. I wouldn't want you to waste any empathy on a woman you've never been able to stand."

*Oh, snap!*

It would figure that Leo would materialize during a show-down that was apparently long overdue. Family loyalty had me straightening my back, even though I was still mad at my mother for several reasons. My defensiveness also came into play because there was something off about Cora Barnes, and I still suspected that she and her husband had something to do with Jacob Blackleach's murder.

"Your mother and I buried the hatchet long ago, but you wouldn't know that, would you? Having run off to the city and all."

"Cora, was there something I could help you with?" I asked, unwilling to allow this confrontation to continue when it was benefitting no one. I felt a manifestation of heat building in my left hand as if I'd pushed off the floor. It was as if a combat sequence was developing in my unconscious mind. In reflection, something of this nature would only have my mother packing my bags without my knowledge and somehow hogtieing and dragging my butt out of town. I needed to restrain myself. "My mom has just arrived into town, and I'd really like to spend some quality time with her."

"I came by to pick up my order." Cora shifted her shoulders, as if that helped her to transition her focus. Her long lashes practically touched her eyebrows and had me wondering if they weren't fake. "I wasn't able to pick it up on Sunday…well, for a number of reasons."

"Of course. Let me go into the back and get that for you." I chanced a worried glance toward my mom, whose laser green eyes appeared to be having a staring contest with the customer. The heat I'd felt in my hand from earlier was waning. It had all been a result of the undertones I'd felt earlier. Cora Barnes was nothing more than a customer—not an enemy. Had she and

Nan truly buried the hatchet? I guess so, considering she was still one of *those* clients. "If you'll excuse me."

I turned fast enough that my green and yellow skirt billowed around my calves. I also managed to catch a bit of orange and black in that mix, deciphering that Leo had been next to me all along.

He'd vanished again, but I had no doubt he would be waiting for me in the storage room.

"Leo, show yourself right now," I commanded in a whisper once I was through the wall of magical fairies warding my storage room entrance, looking everywhere for the fur-balled creature. "I mean it. Or should I call you Benny?"

*What is it that you want?*

Leo materialized next to the tray I'd brought in the other day to organize the orders Nan had put together before her death. The bags were dwindling one by one, leaving only around eight or so behind. This meant I would have to start my training with Leo in the next day or two if I were going to follow in Nan's footsteps. Of course, that could only happen if we found the spell book he'd lost due to his lack of short term memory.

"I need you to remember who killed Jacob Blackleach," I pleaded, easily locating Cora's order on the silver tray. "I still believe that Cora came into the shop, thinking she could meet with me about her purchase. For some reason, she hit Jacob over the head. I'm not sure it was intentional or whether she thought he was some kind of thief."

*Didn't your sheriff say she was at the library?*

"Liam isn't *my* sheriff," I countered, wishing Leo would stay on topic for more than a sentence or two. "Think back, Leo. Was it Cora? What about Otis? I can't imagine him committing murder, but I'm sure that's what everyone says about somebody after they'd been arrested for doing the deed in question. Elsie? Wilma? You know, I keep forgetting Pearl and the man she was with, regardless of her claim that she didn't know who I was talking about. Leo, you were in here last Sunday watching Jacob search for Nan's spell book. You saw the murderer. Can you picture the scene?"

Leo's left eye blinked slowly and the crooked portion of his tail flicked in…remembrance? My hopes began to climb as he remained silent, thinking back to that fateful morning. I ran my fingertips over the fold of the brown paper bag, wishing it were my cell phone. I could call 911, get ahold of Eileen, and have the sheriff arrest Cora right here and now.

*I can smell it…*

"What do you smell? Do you recall inhaling her perfume or Jacob?" I asked, recalling how the Fake Larry always had a peculiar odor about him. "Take a deep breath, Leo, and—"

Leo's bent whiskers pulled up, showing the lower portion of his broken fang, and then…

*Choo! Choo!*

*Ugh. You need to dust in here again.*

Out of all the familiars I could have gotten stuck with, it had to be Leo.

*I take offense at that.*

"Go ahead, take offense," I muttered in defeat, thinking there had to be a spell out there somewhere that could cure short term memory loss. Oh, that's right. I didn't have a spell book, because Leo couldn't remember where Nan had put it before she died while taking a walk. "I'm so screwed."

*I heard that, too. You should be grateful that I'm—*

"Here's your order, Mrs. Barnes," I exclaimed after exiting through the charmed beads. I left Leo in the back room to talk to himself. At least I didn't find my mom and Cora wrestling on the ground about past grudges, but then again, my mom was a witch herself and more than capable of standing on her own two feet. Couldn't she just cast a spell of some sort and have a wart appear on the end of Cora's nose? "That will be fifty dollars."

*We have a lot of work cut out for us if you believe witchcraft can materialize a wart on the end of a person's nose.*

Leo was obviously close by, but I couldn't see him anywhere in the vicinity. And I couldn't know the extent of the witchcraft seeing as I didn't have the spell book, now could I?

*Sarcasm doesn't become you, my dear.*

"Thank you," Cora said somewhat stiffly, slipping a fifty-dollar bill into my hand. The exchange brought about a case of déjà vu. "I'm assuming our order for next week will be available?"

"Yes," I replied, trying to remember what it was that triggered such a weird response.

*It's not easy, is it?*

I ignored Leo, concentrating really hard on Cora and what had just taken place.

That's when my initial altercation with Pearl came back to me in spades. She'd been sneaky about the exchange, almost as if she thought someone would see them. Yet no one else thought anything of purchasing alternative health products from my Nan.

"Cora, have a nice day." I didn't wait for her or my mother to say anything else that would prolong this unwanted reunion. It would do neither woman any good, so I all but escorted the malt shop owner out the door without another word. "Mother, I think I know who killed Jacob Blackleach."

*Here we go again.*

"Would you just be quiet!"

"I didn't say anything, and you need to watch your tone, Raven Lattice Marigold."

"I wasn't talking to you, Mom." I spun around so that my skirt wouldn't hide the scared cretin, though I did understand why Leo would be afraid of my mother's wrath. It was time to get this particular reunion out of the way. "You remember Benny, don't you?"

*I hate you.*

"You secretly love me," I replied to Leo, hoping that was half true. The future ahead of us had the two of us practically attached at the hip, so we'd have to learn to get along at some point. "His name is Leo now, and he's going to help me learn how to be a proper witch."

"I'll deal with you later," Regina warned Leo, who gave what I believe was supposed to be a terrifying hiss. It was a rather pitiful exhale, almost as if he had a hairball, considering the broken fang took away much of the intended effect. "Raven, who do you think killed Jacob Blackleach? And before you answer that, please tell me he had nothing to do with...well, my mother's lifestyle."

*Witchcraft is a lifestyle now? Oh, your mother has been gone to the city for far too long.*

"Mom, Jacob Blackleach was a wizard from Wethersfield, and I think Pearl Saffron somehow figured out that Nan was a real witch. I think Pearl killed Jacob so that no one would figure it out and take away her love potions." It made perfect sense. "All I have to do is figure out a way to convince Liam who the guilty party is without revealing the family secret."

"Curse," my mother countered, crossing her arms and staring

at me as if I wasn't her daughter.

"Gift." Two could play at this game. "Right, Leo?"

*I don't remember.*

## Chapter Twelve

SIX O'CLOCK, THE beginning of the evening's annual trick or treat festivities on River Bay, had arrived some fifty minutes prior. There was still over an hour before the streets would begin to clear, and I was planning to use every minute attempting to come up with a solid motive to explain for Liam why Pearl was the guilty party.

In the interim, I had no choice but to paint a prom queen smile on my face and pretend that my mother's presence didn't bother me in the least.

*I tried the same thing for years. It didn't work.*

"I love the glitter on your wings," I exclaimed, handing over what was essentially a bag of pure refined cane sugar to a little girl dressed up as a butterfly. It appeared that Leo could use a little sweetening up as well. He and my mother had yet to say a word to each other. "Can you really fly between flowers?"

The young girl ran off in a fit of giggles, heading toward Cora Barnes. The woman had been shooting daggers my way since the first trick or treater showed up at my shop's door. I had to fight the urge to send Leo over there incognito to steal her adorable ceramic bowl in shape of a gigantic orange and black jack-o-lantern.

I wouldn't stoop to that level, of course, although I would love to know where Cora had gotten the decorative bowl. I wasn't a dangerous criminal, no matter what some jealous people believed, even after I'd managed to stumble upon a dead body in the back room of *Tea, Leaves, & Eves.*

*No one would ever know it was me.*

"I would know, Leo," I replied with a firm dignity that no one could steal away from me.

*Give her time.*

I ignored Leo's jab regarding my mother's well-known ability to soften my resolve, although I did wonder if she'd ever used witchcraft since leaving Paramour Bay behind. Had she used some small spells on me during my rather obnoxious teenage years? I doubt it, considering she would have done anything to change my mind about going to college.

Didn't that kind of commitment to a choice deserve some respect for her?

*Do you really want me to answer that question?*

"I can't believe that you would dare put that ugly thing on your head," Regina chastised, shooting a frustrated glance underneath the counter at the witch's hat that I'd brought with me from New York. My mom had refused to come near the door as I handed out full-sized bags of Skittles that I'd ordered online for my new shop's offering. I'd wanted everyone to know that I didn't skimp on the treats for Halloween, demonstrating that I was a committed member of the community. Even Cora was only giving out bite-sized Kit-Kats. "You might as well be wearing a sign that declares you're a…"

My mom's voice trailed off, telling me that she couldn't even bring herself to talk about the miraculous gift that had been bestowed on our family. I ignored her, like I'd been doing all afternoon.

Who would have thought that a niche tea shop in such a

small town could do so well? The foot traffic in and out of *Tea,
Leaves, & Eves* had been nonstop, not that I was complaining in
the least. No wonder Fake Larry and Real Larry had said this
place turned a rather nice profit. It made me wonder why Nan
needed to upcharge her so-called homeopathic remedies.

*Hey, those ingredients can get downright expensive and hard to
cultivate.*

A chilly breeze wedged through the glass door I'd propped
open, prompting me to button the neck of my heavy sweater.
The lighter layer of outerwear was conducive to my station, but I
would have needed something heavier had I been outside with
the townsfolk exposed to the late autumn swirling evening
winds.

The town really did it up right.

I couldn't see any of the businesses with their lights out.
Even the volunteer fire department was handing out candy and
neon-colored glow sticks. I'd even set out a high-top table with
small disposable teacups for the parents who'd wanted something
warm to drink, and I was amazed by the outpouring of gratitude
when I'd poured them a fresh cup of Earl Gray directly from the
pot of Earl Gray I had simmering. I figured it was a mild enough
blend that everyone could manage, if nothing more than for the
warmth.

The majority of the town's people were so nice, asking ear-
nest questions with obvious sincerity, unlike the hustle and
bustle of New York City. Everyone there had a destination, and
hardly anyone took the time to talk to one another unless it was
life or death.

The population sign listed Paramour Bay as having three
hundred and fifty-four residents, and I fully believe I'd met most
of them tonight. The masses were now out in force and the

youth were not the only ones in costume. Even some of the adults wore headbands with cat ears and bunny ears, while some of the men had on superhero capes that had the boys and girls either giggling in fun or rolling their eyes in embarrassment for the old tweens.

"You know fully well that I always dressed up as a witch for Halloween," I reminded my mother, dropping another bag of Skittles into a plastic pumpkin. The small boy gave me a toothless grin before walking next door. "The bigger deal you make of this, the higher the likelihood of someone actually taking you seriously."

My own words had me thinking about the correlation I'd made between Pearl Saffron and Jacob Blackleach. I hadn't spotted the purple-haired lady in days. I had to wonder if Liam would check out my theory or if he would shrug it off like he'd done when I thought Cora was the most likely the suspect.

*Let's face it,* Leo offered up with what sounded like optimism, but totally wasn't. *You are on your third accusation. Isn't that kind of like the boy crying wolf? Sooner or later, Liam is going to say enough is enough.*

"Having samples of hot tea out front during this event was a brilliant idea."

*Speak of the devil.*

Liam had inadvertently saved me from arguing with a cat I had no way of winning against…at least at the moment.

"Thank you," I responded, ignoring the tiny flutter of excitement in my heart. I didn't have time for anything other than dealing with the current calamity in my life. "Go ahead. Grab a cup and I'll pour you some, if you'd like. It's pretty chilly out here now that the sun has set."

Liam had wandered up the street, having joined the stream

of trick or treaters as they hit storefront after storefront. He was looking through the display window at my mother, who had a sudden interest in her manicure. It made me question just what type of confrontation these two had over her parking job earlier.

"Did you really give my mother a parking ticket?" I asked, though I softened the accusing tone with a smile. "Or were you pulling my leg?"

*I bet he'd like to pull on something of yours.*

I tried to shove Leo away with my foot, but he'd shifted somewhere where Liam couldn't see him.

"I politely walked across the street today to tell your mother that she couldn't block the alley, which serves as the delivery access point to the back of this row of buildings, but she refused to move her vehicle," Liam shared with me, his dark gaze still settled on my mom. "You might say that things escalated from there until I wasn't given a choice but to write her a parking ticket. Her car is still there, by the way. Midnight begins a new day."

*Ah, midnight. That's when you fully come into your powers. You know, if you're so inclined, you could make those tickets disappear as your first official magic act.*

"I'll make sure she moves her car before then." It was becoming harder and harder to ignore Leo, but Liam's answer did explain why it had been hard for me to see where Mom had been parked, considering the spot had been pretty far down on the right. "I'm so sorry. She can be hard-headed sometimes."

"Don't be sorry." Liam gave me another one of those winks that weakened my knees. "It gave me a chance to visit with you, didn't it?"

*Can I gag now?*

A group of boys and girls kept me from replying to either

Liam or Leo, saving me from making a fool of myself. I longed to get ahold of that spell book, because then I'd be able to cast one that prevented Leo from saying anything that wasn't of absolute importance.

*I take offense at that. Everything I say has importance. And I have a few tricks of my own, you know.*

"Liam, wait," I called out, wanting to run the Pearl thing by him before the night ended. This might be my only chance. "Mom, please take over handing out the Halloween candy and the tea."

I didn't wait for my mother to come to the door, because I'd probably be there until the end of the time. She wanted nothing to do with anything in this town, but she was going to have to accept that I'd made my choice.

Paramour Bay was now my home.

At least, for the foreseeable future.

I quickly left the basket on the ground, giving her no choice but to take over the candy duty. In moments, I'd caught up with Liam.

"Could I speak to you regarding the Jacob Blackleach case?"

"Sure," Liam replied, seemingly somewhat surprised when I fell into step beside him and put my arm through his. It just seemed natural to preserve heat between us as we spoke. Of course, I had to wait until we'd walked past Cora before going into further detail. "You should know that Detective Swanson called me today. The ledger he took into evidence seems to have been misplaced. Now, I don't want you to worry. He's an upstanding detective, and I can promise you that he will do everything in his power to locate the evidence bag and determine what happened to the chain of custody. I was going to tell you tomorrow, because I didn't want to ruin your birthday and the

Halloween gathering tonight."

Wow, did I feel bad about that particular situation.

It wasn't like I could tell him that Leo had taken the ledger or that it was in my possession. Besides, I was a horrible liar. Terrible. Yet, I found myself lying more and more. I would eventually have to stop, but for now, I nodded my head in commiseration.

"I appreciate that you were looking out for my best interest." Had that sounded genuine? I wasn't sure, so I kept talking to smooth things over. "I'm sure that Detective Swanson will find the ledger sooner or later. Listen, while we're on the subject, I was thinking that you might want to look into Pearl."

"Pearl? Really?"

I could hear the skepticism in Liam's voice loud and clear. Leo's analogy of the boy crying wolf came to mind, but I ignored it just as fast. It was best I follow up with the reasoning for my suspicion.

"Do you remember me coming to the diner on Monday when I thought that maybe Larry had something to do with Jacob's murder?"

Liam glanced sideways at me, letting me know full well he recalled me interrupting his lunch. It probably wasn't my best idea to bring up the fact that I'd accused someone else besides Larry and Cora.

This conversation was not going the way I'd hoped.

"Raven, Pearl is in her mid-seventies. I highly doubt that she had the strength to render a man the size of Jacob Blackleach unconscious."

"And I would have agreed with you had I not thought back to her reaction the day she came into the store to buy the love potion Nan had mixed up for her. And what if she had the element of surprise and hit him from behind? You said yourself that half the town used Nan for her homeopathic remedies, but what if Pearl thought that Nan was a real witch? I'm telling you that she was acting very strange that day, almost as if we were making some secret sordid deal that no one knew about...but they did! You said so yourself." I couldn't stop myself from wincing at the thought that Leo was going to come out of nowhere and swipe at my ankles for bringing up Nan and witchcraft in the same sentence. I'd taken to wearing boots every day, though that had more to do with the colder season than Leo's physical assaults. "Pearl had been standing across the street and watching the storefront when I'd arrived in town. And she did the same thing the majority of the day on Monday morning until she'd worked up the courage to come inside the shop to get her order. What if she thought Jacob was there to steal the recipes Nan used for those tea leaves? What if she thought she'd lose her secret love potion?"

I was purposefully talking about homeopathic remedies and tea leaves to throw Liam off the witchcraft trail, but I wasn't technically lying, either.

That was good, right?

Including a bit of the truth in each deliberate lie was the best course of action.

"Look, Raven, I understand your need to solve a murder that has put a sort of tarnish on your recent move to Paramour Bay," Liam said after having stopped in front of the small grocery store two blocks down from the tea shop. He even gave me an understanding smile, though I tried not to take offense that he was treating me with kid gloves. His reaction made me want to scream the truth from the rooftops. "I really do, but Detective Swanson is still leaning toward Blackleach being here in town because of Larry and his estate business. I'm inclined to agree with him. It makes more sense."

It was a struggle for me not to reveal the supernatural elements to this case, but it was in my best interest to keep a low profile—for now. All I could do was try one more time to talk Liam into looking at Pearl as a viable suspect.

"Please. At least interview her," I asked imploringly, resting my hand on his forearm. I hadn't meant to touch him any more than I had, but it came almost naturally. After all, he'd given me coffee as a birthday gift. "And if you come away with the same opinion of her innocence as you have now, then I'll drop it."

It wouldn't be that easy, but another white lie in the midst of so many couldn't hurt at this point, right?

"Pearl usually stays away from the annual trick or treating event because it's too chaotic for her, but I promise that I'll drop by her place tomorrow," Liam conceded with a shake of his head, as if he couldn't believe he'd agreed to such a task. My chest warmed at the thought that he was doing something special just for me and me alone. "You should get back to your shop. I've heard there's a bit of a feud still brewing between your mom and Cora Barnes."

"You know about that?" I asked, somewhat shocked that Liam would be so well-versed on that type of history when I hadn't even thought about my mother's life here over thirty years ago. "Did something specific happen to garner such intense hatred?"

"I've heard a tale or two from Otis, but nothing concrete." Liam had certainly sidestepped that question, hadn't he? "I'll be making another round or two before the night is through. I'll see you in a bit."

The rich scent of burning firewood drifted over from some

of the houses along the lake in the neighborhood to the south of us. I inhaled deeply, appreciating the autumn aroma that one didn't get to smell in the city. The small groups of older kids raced past the younger ones and their escorts. It was straight out of the Normal Rockwell collection—the typical American Halloween night with all its commercial and celebratory promise.

Despite the murder, witchcraft, and the feud between my mother and I, it was a beautiful autumn evening for this Halloween. Children's mischievous laughter floated through the air, the feeling of unity throughout the town was palpable, and the close-knit community of Paramour Bay was vividly alive as its residents joined together in the festive holiday.

Would I have been different had I grown up here instead of New York City?

Could I have been one of those carefree children?

*Do you really need me to answer that question?*

Leo would certainly have livened up my life in some aspect, though I highly doubt he was as sarcastic then as he was now. I glanced down to find that he was weaving in and out of the fabric of my skirt.

"Were you afraid to leave me alone for one minute with Liam?" I asked in a soft tone that only he could hear. Technically, I supposed he could read my mind, but that just gave me the heebie-jeebies. "I handled it, Leo."

*I actually came to collect you because something bad is about to happen…* Leo lifted his bent whiskers and inhaled deeply. *Is that fish from the diner?*

"Focus, Leo." I bent down to look him in the larger eye, not caring now who saw me talking to a cat that somewhat resembled roadkill. For Leo to say something bad was about to happen…well, that was exceptionally bad. "Tell me. What do you mean something bad is about to happen?"

# Chapter Thirteen

"MOM!" I PLOWED through another group of children milling about on the sidewalk, ignoring the rude looks I was getting from their parents. I might be upset with my mother, but that didn't mean I wanted anything to happen to her during her visit. Not even a glare from Cora Barnes prevented me from sprinting past her shop until I'd skidded to a stop in the doorway of *Tea, Leaves, & Eves*. "Mom! Mom, is everything okay?"

"Of course, it isn't," Regina muttered, shoving the basket of Skittles into my hand as if the handle was on fire. Her scowl was worse than Cora's grimace. "You won't listen to reason. We need to leave this town, Raven. Tonight, before midnight."

I managed to exhale slowly at the knowledge that nothing bad had occurred while I'd left the shop to speak with Liam. Nothing in the store seemed out of place, and the street was still choked with trick or treaters wanting their sugar fix.

Everything was status quo.

"I've already told you that I'm not leaving all of this behind." A chorus of *trick or treat, smell my feet* rang out. I pasted a smile on my face as I spun around and dutifully handed out the bags of candy. Leo had been wrong. Nothing bad had happened. "Mom, I'm staying. I'm not only going to live here for the next twelve months or more, but I'm also going to learn everything I can about our family ancestry. I really, really wish you'd support me this once."

My mother didn't even bother to put on platitudes for the children and their parents stopping by for their Halloween treats. Her green eyes practically glowed as her irritation mounted, but I was no longer cowered by her antics.

"You could help me, if you wanted," I suggested, truly believing I'd learn more from her than Leo. I waited for some sarcastic remark from the old ruffian, but his silence told me that he agreed. Unless, of course, he'd gone off in search of that fish and couldn't hear a word of this conversation. "Whatever you and Nan argued about doesn't matter now, Mom. She's not here to cause you any more pain."

For the first time since hearing about Nan's death, tears surfaced in my mother's eyes. Guilt slammed into me upon seeing unspoken grief consume a daughter who'd lost her mother. It was easy to forget due to my mom's ability to compartmentalize her life. She had a lot of pent-up issues.

I instantly stepped forward, wrapping an arm around her shoulders.

"Oh, Mom. I didn't mean to make you cry."

"No, I'm fine," Regina protested, though her actions suggested otherwise. She held onto me in a tight embrace, sniffling and swiping away her tears. I could literally count on one hand the times I'd seen this woman cry. That lone reality made me pull her even closer. "Really, I'm fine. I just think back to all the quality time we missed out on because of her stubborn ways. Your Nan was so hardheaded."

I couldn't help but smile at my mother's tenacity to hold onto past grudges, because it was evident where she'd gotten her obstinate ways. Regina still managed to somehow distance herself by calling Rosemary my Nan instead of her mother.

"Trick or treat!"

"Go. Give those adorable creatures candy." Regina shooed me away while attempting to fix her makeup. She'd always hated getting emotional, and today was no exception. "And we'll not discuss this again. The past needs to stay in the past, before it's too late."

It took all my might not to roll my eyes at the effort she'd put back into trying to get me to see things her way. Regina Marigold wasn't the type of woman to give up on anything easily, and I was proud to say that particular trait ran in the family.

I wouldn't give up on our family, either.

To say I felt optimistic about my future was an understatement. This was the first time we'd connected on an emotional level in a really long time.

I didn't doubt that Mom would continue to try and convince me to return to New York City, but I wouldn't allow myself to cave in my determination to learn what Nan never had a chance to teach me. I had Leo and Ted in my corner, and a lot of caring customers who wanted the tea shop to succeed.

And Liam.

He was a special kind of man.

What else was there to say about the attractive sheriff, other than he made my heart flutter every time he graced me with his smile?

That left Heidi, and it tore at my heart that it wasn't the best of ideas to tell her that I was a witch. She was my best friend. How could I possibly keep something this important from her?

The answer was simple.

I couldn't.

I would have to find a way to tell her what was happening in my life. However, it had to be in a way that didn't jeopardize what Nan had built here in Paramour Bay.

In the meantime, I still had candy to hand out, and Liam had a murder to solve.

Who was I kidding?

*We* had a murder to solve, and he needed me.

I wanted to help in our endeavor, especially considering Jacob Blackleach had been a wizard trying to steal Nan's spell book. Liam couldn't know about that little fact.

The rest of the hour passed by quickly, allowing me to meet more of the residents and their families. This small Connecticut town had been so welcoming, and I'd learned quite a bit about Nan's life here, such as her love of the book club and her affinity to the wax museum. I'm still not so sure why such an odd place had captured her heart, but it was something I could ask Leo about at a later date.

Speaking of which, I hadn't seen him in quite a while.

That fish he'd been hungry for must have been really good.

"Cora Barnes looks at least ten years younger than I do," my mother mumbled, having taken a small compact mirror out of her purse as I was closing up the shop. I carried the tray back inside that still held a stack of leftover disposable cups and the carafe of the pumpkin spice flavored tea. The only thing left outside was the high-top table, which was extremely light due to the metal being black powder coated cast aluminum. "I wonder if that was my mother's doing."

I didn't have the heart to tell my mom that she was absolutely correct in that assumption. I'd seen in the ledger that she drank a special tea that contained a variation of a Celtic youth spell I had yet to study up on. According to Leo, it wouldn't keep her young for all eternity, but it would manage to shed five or ten years during her aging process. At least, as long as she cared for a miniature live oak tree she had in her possession and continued to drink the concoction. Oddly enough, she was required to pour out the last few drops of each daily cup onto the roots of the tiny shrub and chant a few ancient Gaelic words.

"Well, you can't act like it's something you couldn't do if you wanted to," I suggested, storing the table off to the side until morning. I'd already seen the response Leo gave me when talking about using magic for oneself. It would be interesting to witness my mother's reaction. "You have all the required tools at your disposal, right?"

"Did Benny not talk to you about the consequences of abjuration magic?" Regina asked, snapping shut the compact mirror in horror. "Raven, dear, you can never—and I mean never—use magic to alter your own destiny. The ramifications are just...well, don't do it. You've seen the cat."

"Then I guess you'll have to help guide me, won't you?"

It was rare that I managed to get my mother in a corner, but this was definitely one of those sporadic moments that I would totally take advantage of before she could wiggle her way out of it.

"I will not—"

"So you're going to just sit back and allow me to dabble in spells and witchcraft, knowing full well there could be unknown consequences for my actions due to my family's negligence in seeing to my proper training?"

*Oh, you're good.*

"Raven Lattice Marigold."

"Leo, where have you been?" I asked, ignoring my mother's pronouncement of my full name. It had taken awhile, but I was glad she was here to celebrate my birthday. We'd always have cake and a bottle of wine, usually joined by Heidi. We could always FaceTime her when we got back to the house, though I was still wary of engaging in a conversation with her where I might let it slip I had been born into a family of witches. "I was getting worried a dog got to you or something."

I really wasn't, but I'd rather talk to him than continuing the conversation with my mother.

*I went to find that fish, but I ended up at the library.*

"Benny, stop worrying about eating fish and start looking after my daughter," Regina said before she began pacing in front of the counter. "I've tried every which way to get her to see reason, but only you can tell her how she'll end up old, alone, and shackled with the role of the odd eccentric cat lady who lives on the edge of town."

*That's Mr. Leo to you. The part of me that was Benny—and how glorious he was—passed on to the other side with your mother, bless their souls.*

"Wait, you can hear Leo?" I was confused, seeing as Ted couldn't hear Nan's familiar. "I thought only I could hear him."

"Unfortunately, anyone in the Marigold bloodline can hear that cretin. I ignored him earlier, because I'd hoped to be back in New York City by now."

*Take that back. I'm not a cretin. I saved your hide a time or two, now didn't I, missy?*

"Would you two please stop?" I exclaimed, resting my hands on my hips to show them I wasn't messing around. "Today is my birthday, and I'd like to end it on a peaceful note and a bottle of red."

*Well, you should have thought about that before you gave Cora Barnes only part of her order. She's about to make an entrance in three, two, one...*

"Raven, I'm going to assume you didn't realize you'd made a mistake with my order." Sure enough, Cora came through the glass door like a tornado. The scent of her rather musky perfume hit me first, if that were even possible. "There wasn't nearly enough in this bag to cover what I paid for earlier."

Leo swooshed his bent tail in satisfaction that he was right about Cora's reason for barging into the shop after hours. He sashayed his way toward the storage room, giving my mother a sideways glance of satisfaction that he hadn't caved to her will. It didn't take a genius to figure out that she was about to chase him the rest of the way.

"I'm so sorry," I apologized, trying to be sincere about my mistake, all the while covering up the brewing argument between a witch and a cat. Cora made it rather hard for me to be genuine with the way her accusing eyes were focused directly on me as if I'd burnt down her shop. "I'll—"

*That can be arranged. It's just a flick of a kitchen match.*

"Shut up," Regina snapped at Leo, obviously having been out of practice at the fact that familiars continued to talk without regular humans hearing the conversation. Unfortunately, Cora instantly assumed that my mother had lashed out at her given her understanding of the context. "Now, Cora, I wasn't—"

"If you think for a second that you and your daughter can waltz into this town and take it over as if you never left, you have another think coming, Regina Marigold." Cora's cheeks had flushed in anger way past the capability of her makeup to disguise. This wasn't a situation I was going to be able to smooth over. "I had a business arrangement with Rosemary, and I expect Raven here to honor that agreement. You have nothing to do with it, so you mind your own business."

"Mom, why don't you go in the back room while I take care of this business transaction?" My mind was like a tsunami with every thought crashing in my mind on how to charm my way out of the upcoming confrontation. My training as a receptionist came back tenfold—the caller was always right. Isn't that the same phrase used in retail? The customer was always right. "Cora, my apologies. I must not have seen the additional bags Nan had set aside."

For once, my mother must have realized the trouble she'd caused me with her outburst. She silently left the main area of the shop and slipped past the protective string of ivory-colored fairies. Her compliant behavior told me that she took our heritage seriously, and understood how important it was to keep our magical powers hidden away from the world.

"You're new." Cora feigned the process of picking an invisible piece of lint off the sleeve of her dress. It was very hard to like a woman who thought herself better than others due to her station in life. I was honestly surprised that Nan continued to take her orders, unless Cora had respect for Rosemary Marigold…unlike the obvious distain she displayed for her protégés. "Mistakes are bound to happen."

"Yes, they are." Seeing as there had only been eight bags or so left on the tray, I'd stored them underneath the cash register in a locked cabinet. The brief walk to grab them gave me the time to phrase my next statement. I wanted it to be clear that I wasn't my grandmother. Whatever social understanding they had died with Nan. No one spoke to my mother in such a disrespecting manner. Well, except Leo, but there was nothing I could do to erase that bad blood. "My one mistake was not conducting this latest business as I saw fit."

Sure enough, there were two other brown bags with Cora's

name written on them. I'd picked them up before finishing my sentence, which gave me the distinct pleasure of seeing the woman's expression of caution.

*You go, girl.*

Leo must not have wanted to be with my mother in the back room. He rounded the counter with me, though Cora's squinted gaze was solely on me.

"I don't know the history between you and my mother, nor do I know what arrangement you and my grandmother had regarding your orders. There is one thing I can tell you for certain, and that is that you and I won't be doing business anymore due to your unkind disposition." I held out the two bags for Cora to take from my grasp. "Have a good night, Mrs. Barnes."

"You...you can't do that," Cora protested even while taking the bags from hand. "We need this special tea."

*Yada, yada, yada. Whine, whine, whine. The clients are all the same when they no longer have access to the one thing they want—magic.*

"And had you welcomed me to town the way everyone else has done, then maybe we could have continued doing business in a polite and civil manner," I pointed out, recalling very well our first encounter at the diner. Even Flo had mentioned Cora's rude behavior stemming from her family's money. "But you'll have to buy your special blend of *tea* elsewhere."

Cora obviously wanted to protest my decision, but she gave a small huff and walked out the door without another word. I'd never been too good at confrontation, so my hands were still trembling.

*You know that she'll be back, right? Just wait until she notices that first wrinkle in the mirror.*

"Then it better be with a sincere apology." Although I would somehow have to make sure my mother did the same, considering it had been rude of her to shout the words *shut up* for all to hear. "Cora Barnes hasn't been nice to me since she first met me at the diner earlier this week. I do feel bad about not giving Desmond his tea blend."

Out of everyone I'd met in this town, I'd been so sure that the person responsible for hitting Jacob Blackleach over the head was Cora Barnes. She was the only one mean enough to do that sort of thing.

*Desmond? Why would you think Desmond drinks that stuff?*

"Doesn't he?" Leo was giving the ivory-colored fairies a sideways glance, as if making sure my mother wasn't about to materialize through the strands. "Cora kept saying *we* when talking about who the tea was for."

*My dear Raven, the magical blend was for Cora Barnes' auxiliary group. Those women are obsessed with their youth. You should have seen—*

To say that Leo's left eye was on the verge of popping out of its socket was an understatement. It was as if I were watching a cartoon. You know, when one of the animated characters' eyes zoom in and out on something crazy.

"Leo, what it is it?"

*I remember who killed Jacob Blackleach. Oh, this is bad. Really bad.*

"Who? And what's so bad? Remembering?"

Leo had me so confused with his confession that I took a step closer to him to see if I could comfort him. I came up short when the bell above the door rang out, but I didn't turn around right away to see who it was…because this ominous dark energy surrounded me until I was almost choking to breathe.

The person responsible for Jacob Blackleach's death had just walked into my tea shop. Of that, I was drop dead certain.

Leo bared his teeth and hissed while rising up on his claws, bending his body until his back was arched higher than his head. His hostile reaction told me that he was fearful about what was about to take place.

*Yes! And there's a reason for that, Raven. You don't know any magic. We're doomed. We're all going to die. I'm going to die looking like a monstrosity that was almost certainly Frankenstein's best friend.*

# *Chapter Fourteen*

"FLO."

I somehow gathered the courage to turn around after saying the murderer's name, still unable to connect the friendly waitress to the persona of a cold-blooded killer. The redhead stood really close to the door, making it all but impossible for me to take that route to safety.

There was an exit out back, but I'm not sure I could make it that far without Flo reaching me first. And what if she had a weapon?

*A gun? You know, I can sneak out and try to lure the sheriff over this way. I'm sure he's still outside somewhere, making sure that everyone made it safely to their vehicles.*

I didn't bother to respond to Leo's panic, knowing full well he could easily slip away without being seen. He could disappear at will, yet the terror this situation invoked seemed to have him forgetting that particular gift.

My mother, on the other hand, was still in the back room. Hopefully, she'd heard the exchange between me and Leo. She could dial 911 and get ahold of Eileen.

*Not if Regina doesn't have her cell phone. It's over on the counter. Oh, and Heidi's called you both numerous times. You might want to take care of that little problem later.*

"Raven, Cora was just telling me that you're no longer going to be making us our special little blend of tea. You can't do that. Seriously, I've never looked better. I even got Albert to notice me at the diner the other day. What will it take for you to continue to make the tea for us? What is it that you want?"

Flo's voice sounded different than the day she'd welcomed me to town or offered me tea at the diner, yet I would have recognized the slight remnant of her Southern accent anywhere. She must have moved here from the south at some point in her life, not that it mattered right this minute. I was about to die, because I hadn't practiced any magic.

*So am I!* As if a flip had switched, Leo had remembered his ability to appear and disappear at will. *Oh, wait. I can leave. I'll go get help. Stall her as long as you can.*

"You're right. I'm not doing business with Cora anymore, although I didn't realize that you were drinking Nan's special tea, as well," I said as casually as possible. There was no way for Flo to know that I had this newfound ability to sense auras, nor could she realize that I'd figured everything out. I needed to play along as if I was clueless to give Leo or my mother a chance to get help. "You said yourself that Cora isn't the nicest woman, but maybe you and I can come to some sort of mutually beneficial arrangement."

Flo regarded me carefully as she tried to gauge if I was being sincere. I slowly walked over to the counter, feigning the need to write her order down on a piece of paper. If I could reach the cash register, then my mother's phone should be in plain sight.

"Stop."

I did my best to give Flo an inquisitive glance as to why she would want me to impede my progress, though I had made it to the front of the small counter. My expression wasn't going to be enough to get her to believe me, so I plucked the feathered pen out of its holder.

"Is there a problem? I'm certain you and I can come to an agreement, as long as I can leave Cora out of this. I really don't want to be working with someone who dislikes my family as much as she seems to loathe us."

"Where is your mother?" Flo asked hesitantly, her gaze darting toward the ivory-colored fairies. "I saw her handing out candy to the children earlier. Where has she gotten off to?"

"Mom drove back to my house," I replied with ease, though it was becoming harder and harder to keep up this pretense. "As you can imagine, it was a long day for her. And the sheriff wanted the alley she'd parked in front of cleared before midnight."

I tensed when Flo looked out the display window, but I was relatively sure that she couldn't see far enough down the street in the darkness to tell whether or not my mother's car was still parked in front of the alley's access ramp.

"I'm tired myself," I replied, feigning a large yawn while covering my mouth with the back of my hand. "You know, we can always talk about this tomorrow."

"Why were you talking with the sheriff tonight?"

And this was where things were going to start unfolding, because it was more than evident that guilt over killing an innocent man had gotten to Flo. Yes, I might have been talking to Liam about who I believed had murdered Jacob Blackleach, but I'd been way off base.

Everything fell into place now that I looked back on this week's events.

When I'd first met Flo at the diner, she'd mentioned that Cora had been aging right along with the rest of them. At the time, it had seemed like such a harmless comment, but she had been testing the ground. Then when Candy and Dee had been talking about the murder, Candy had revealed that Detective Swanson had been around town showing Jacob Blackleach's picture and that Flo had been the only one to recognize him while everyone else couldn't pick him out of the crowd.

Connecting Flo to Cora's group of women had been the icing on the missing element.

Well, my newfound ability to sense auras had technically been the decisive element, but I suppose I'd have to categorize my power as the determining factor—because right now my chest was burning with the realization that I needed to get away from this woman. And right now. The heat in my left palm was back, giving me a strange sensation.

"Did you know that Liam gave my mother a parking ticket?" I asked, managing to take another step back so that my hip was lined up with the side of the counter. Sure enough, I could literally see my mother's phone next to the cash register. "I couldn't believe it, either. I was trying to talk him into ripping up the ticket, but he sure is a stickler for the law."

*Crash!*

Both Flo and myself whipped our heads to the side in alarm, especially when I could hear my mother muttering a few choice words at Leo. I thought he'd gone in search of Liam, but he must have forgotten his destination. I chanced a glance toward Flo, whose expression had gone from startled to angry in a matter of seconds.

Oh, this wasn't good. Not at all.

"Look at that," I said in a forced upbeat tone, quickly swiping my mother's phone off the counter. "My mother must have come back to the shop to help me close up. Wasn't that sweet of her?"

"You know, don't you?"

Another round of déjà vu visited me in the span of a day. Hadn't my mother said those same exact words earlier this morning?

"I don't know what you're accusing me of," I swiftly denied as panic blossomed throughout my body. My fight or flight instinct took over. I have to admit, flight was winning by a mile. "Oh, wait. You're talking about your order. Of course, I know how to make the tea blend. Can't you tell?"

I tilted my face, hoping that the lighting in the shop shone just right on my skin. I'd found a new wrinkle or two around my eyes this morning, but wasn't that expected at the age of thirty?

Flo hastily backtracked to where the light switch was located near the front door. The shop descended into darkness. Well, not total darkness. The streetlights from the sidewalk illuminated the main area, and my sight adjusted accordingly. It appeared that my attempt at stalling her had petered out.

I tried really hard not to take offense that she didn't believe I'd used Nan's aging potion.

"You know very well that it was me who killed Jacob Black-leach."

Had Flo just admitted to being a murderer?

It would have helped had I been able to see Flo's expression clearly, but that obviously wasn't going to happen.

*Dial 911! Your mother is working on something to stop her from killing us.*

"All you had to do was go and get Liam," I muttered harshly, taking a step back as Flo's silhouette came closer. "You still have time. Go!"

"Who are you talking to?" Flo asked, though she sounded as flustered as I did. "Don't you move! I need to explain to you why I had to kill that man. I didn't have a choice!"

*Is she serious?*

"Leo, go now!" I couldn't believe he was still here when I was about to fight for my life. One step back and another to the right put the counter and cash register between me and the killer. "Flo, let's go talk to Liam. You can tell him what happened in detail. I'm sure you acted in self-defense."

*Self-defense? Did you see her beady little eyes? I'm pretty sure the murder was intentional.*

"Who's Leo?" Flo was now close enough to touch the cash register, but far enough that I could still maneuver to the left or right without her catching me. I just had to decide which way to run. "Raven, dear, you need to understand that the man was going to steal all the orders. That's why he was here. I saw him enter the tea shop and had to do something before he got away with everything."

"See? It sounds like self-defense to me," I encouraged her, pressing the home button on my mother's phone. "Are you kidding me?"

*Let me guess. Passcode?*

"I'm not kidding you," Flo replied imploringly to my philosophical question regarding my mom's habit of changing passwords every week. She was slightly paranoid, and now that I'd been let in on the family secret, I totally understood why. "He was going to steal your grandmother's tea blends. I couldn't let him do that. You need them. We need them. I cannot get any more wrinkles, don't you understand? I finally got Albert to notice me, and I wasn't about to let some stranger come in here and take away the only thing that truly works for me."

"Flo, you don't need to look younger to have a man notice you."

*Good advice. Have you seen Albert? His wrinkles are deeper than the Atlantic Ocean.*

"Hush it," I muttered, wishing he'd stop putting in his two cents. "Flo, you took a man's life. You didn't just stop a burglary."

"A bad man who was going to steal from your grandmother," Flo stated, her entire attitude changing in a blink of an eye. She took a step forward, indicating she was about to come around the counter. I instinctively responded to her movement in kind. "I can't let you ruin everything. If you won't make that magical blend Rosemary was able to do, then I'll have to do it myself."

*She just threatened you.*

"Did you just threaten my daughter?"

*Oh, boy. This is going to be good.*

The flash bang that came out of nowhere garnered a scream that was louder than the time Liam had knocked on my car door window. Leo hadn't given me enough warning, so I instinctively ducked down and covered my head with my arms, hoping whatever had happened didn't kill me.

*Would you look at that? Your mother still has the same old pizzazz.*

The tea shop was suddenly flooded with light, courtesy of my mother. She was standing by the light switch with a very satisfied smile on her face. As a matter of fact, the only time I remembered an expression like that was when a boy crashed his bike into a tree after he'd called me a name that I couldn't repeat and—

"You made Randy Clark crash his bike into a tree back in seventh grade!"

"I don't know what you're talking about," Regina denied emphatically, nodding toward the floor where the smoke was gradually dissipating from the air. I peered over the counter to find that Flo had fallen to the floor in a heap and appeared to be sleeping peacefully. "Now this…well, this was definitely my doing. You can thank me for saving your life later, after you've packed your bags and we're both on our way out of this miserable little town."

*And to think a sliver of pride had slipped in underneath my loathing.*

Leo's lip lifted to show his broken fang in disgust toward Regina.

"Mom, I'm not leaving…even after all of this." I slowly edged my way around the counter, wondering what kind of spell my mother had cast to get Flo to sleep this deeply. I have to admit, I was really impressed with Mom's abilities, considering that she'd left this life behind. "What is your password? I need to call—"

*Look at that. It's like the good sheriff somehow knew you needed him.*

Sure enough, Liam was standing at the glass door with his brown eyes focused solely on Flo, who was still lying in a heap on the ground. I figured that absolute shock was traveling through his system at the scene in front of him, but his NYPD training must have been darn good.

He didn't bat an eye.

Flo must have flipped the deadbolt on the door, so my mother sighed audibly as she flicked her wrist and let Liam come into the shop.

"Raven, what happened?" Liam asked, rushing to Flo's side while pulling his cell phone out of the front pocket of his shirt. "Did Flo have a heart attack? Was she sick? Did she faint?"

"Yes," I exclaimed, grabbing onto the last excuse he offered.

Liam would never understand this bizarre world I'd stepped into long before I'd ever realized it. He needed protection, and it was my responsibility to ensure that the underworld of witchcraft didn't invade Paramour Bay. "Flo fainted, right after I told her I was calling 911 to let you know that she confessed to murdering Jacob Blackleach."

# *Chapter Fifteen*

"**H**EIDI, THANK YOU so much. You have no idea how much I needed this."

*This* was five fresh ground pounds of my favorite cinnamon flavored coffee from the best café in New York City. Well, at least I thought so. I bent the tabs on the top of the white bag before opening it and inhaling the delicious aroma that literally made me salivate.

How had I gone two weeks without this delectable beverage?

Tea could never replace my chosen brew, and it made me think that maybe I could include specialty coffees on the shelves of my shop. That way, I could infuse the beans with the same spells combined with the tea leaves.

I waited to hear some sarcastic reply from Leo, but he was unusually quiet today. It was hard not to look around my kitchen for the orange and black ruffian that I'd come to rely on more than I would have thought possible.

"I saw Ted walking into town," Heidi said, taking a seat on one of the stools at the counter. She was dressed casually in jeans with her blonde hair pulled back in a ponytail. I'd seen her glancing around the house a time or two, most likely looking for the furball she'd sworn she saw that last time she was here. I truly hoped she didn't bring it up, because I didn't doubt for a second she'd recognize my lies. "Does he not drive? I've got to tell you,

I've been worried sick about you being all alone this far out here with him. I mean, we don't know a thing about that guy."

I took my time pouring the grounds into the generic coffee maker I'd stuffed into the trunk of my vehicle the day I'd moved to Paramour Bay. It hadn't crossed my mind that having such a device in a tea shop might not be the best business decision, but my new home was now my sanctuary.

I could indulge my habit.

I could have all the coffee I wanted, though I still couldn't convince Ted to have a cup. As a matter of fact, I don't think I'd ever seen Ted eat or drink anything in the weeks we'd known each other.

"Ted likes to walk into town to visit Mindy," I explained, wiggling my eyebrows and doing my best to get Heidi talking about Patrick. The two of them had apparently hit a rough patch. He had a tendency to pick his teeth with anything he could find…including one of her business cards. I choked back a gag as I hit the brew button. "Was that Patrick who called earlier?"

Heidi had arrived into town last night with an overnight bag in hand. We'd enjoyed a bottle of wine while I did my best to steer the conversation toward her love life and away from anything to do with me.

Remember, I was a really bad liar.

It had worked for the most part, but I ended up having to go into more detail regarding Flo Akers and her obsession with looking younger than her sixty-one years. There had been no need for Liam or the state police detective who he'd called in to make the arrest to know the entire truth.

Flo had awakened without ever really knowing how she'd fainted to begin with, and began spouting off to anyone who would listen that she'd done the town a favor by ridding it of an evil man who was going to steal Nan's herbal remedies from everyone.

Detective Swanson's case had been wrapped up with a red bow, and Liam had graciously given me and my mother all the credit in uncovering the identity of the murderer.

All's well that ends well, right?

At least, that's what I kept telling myself.

"No, it was your mother who called," Heidi replied, picking a grape off the stems I'd set in a fruit bowl on the counter. She was watching me a little too carefully, so I turned and opened the cabinet where Nan had kept her cups. There were two travel mugs, both of them decorated with little steaming teacups, but they would easily hide the evidence of coffee. "She called me when you didn't answer your cell phone. Wanted me to remind you that she's coming to visit on Wednesday. I've got to say I'm surprised Regina's had such a change of heart regarding you staying in this cute little town."

"Oh, you know my mother," I countered with a dismissive wave of my hand as my heart warmed at the thought that she was slowly becoming okay with my decision to stay in Paramour Bay. "She's like a tornado. Picks a fight here, and it ends with something entirely different over there. Honestly, I think it's great that she reconnected with some of her old high school friends."

"You mean that Cora Barnes?" Heidi scrunched her nose in distaste. "Regina told me all about that woman. Are you still holding out on making her that tea?"

My mother and I had come to an agreement to tell Heidi as much of the truth as possible—and that included the herbal remedies my Nan had been selling on the side. It did explain a lot, and it went a long way in including Heidi in on a piece of my life that encompassed a part of who I was.

"Absolutely." Now that I think about it, there was something else I could be truthful about regarding this new life I was living. "Did I tell you about the stray cat that showed up?"

*Don't you dare.*

It took all of my might not to smile at Leo's voice in my head. The little stinker had been here all along.

"Stray cat?" Heidi spun around on her stool, looking in every nook and cranny of the kitchen and living room. "I love kittens! How old? Wait. I didn't see a kitty in the house last night when we were drinking wine."

"Maybe that's because we *were* drinking wine," I said with a laugh, wondering if I could coax Leo into showing himself. "And this handsome fellow comes and goes as he pleases. He has a bit of an attitude, but I think that's because of all the hardships he's faced in his life."

*Attitude? Hardships?*

"Did I mention handsome? You'll just have to look past all of his battle scars."

I was getting really good at answering other people, all the while addressing Leo. Granted, he could hear my thoughts—which was downright creepy—but I couldn't force myself to engage in conversation with him in that manner.

"Oh, that poor thing." Heidi began to blow kisses and murmur sweet nothings to entice the cat out from hiding. "Here, kitty, kitty, kitty. Here, kitty, kitty, kitty."

*I hate you.*

Leo finally emerged from around the coffee table, eliciting a gasp of surprise from Heidi. She had a bad habit of being brutally honest, but that didn't mean she lacked a heart of gold.

Leo had been strutting his stuff, sashaying his crooked tail back and forth. It was as if he'd been born into royalty, and he was showing the world for all to see. In this moment, he was the Persian leopard he'd always fantasized about in his dreams.

*What is she doing? Raven? Tell her to stop.*

"Oh, Raven, look at the poor thing," Heidi consoled, picking up Leo as if he were any other ordinary housecat. "You come right here to your Aunt Heidi."

I guess because of who Leo was and the role he played in my life, I'd never considered petting him or picking him up to show my affection. And affection was really a strong word, because the two of us butted heads worse than any sibling rivalry.

*I'm going to vanish. Right now. If she doesn't put me down, I'm going to disappear into thin air, and then the rest of the human world will know you're a witch.*

Leo would do no such thing, because though he had the worst attitude any cat could ever have, his loyalty was unwavering. It was kind of humorous to watch Heidi rub her cheek on top of Leo's head while scratching her fingernails underneath his chin. He could protest all he wanted, but the loud purr coming from his rather disheveled body said something else entirely.

"Leo really likes to be scratched on the belly and—"

A knock came at the front door, prompting Leo to take advantage of the moment and leap out of Heidi's arms. True to his word, he did disappear, but in such a way that Heidi believed he'd run up the spiral staircase to the loft above.

"Can you pour our coffees to go?" I walked around the island and toward the front door, leaving Heidi to brush off the fur that had come off onto her shirt. "Ted must have returned home. I'll see what he needs."

The only one who's ever knocked before was Ted, so I certainly wasn't expecting Liam to be standing on my front step. His gaze appeared glued to the side of the house, and from his expression, he was clearly mystified as to why Nan had allowed so many vines to grow wild.

I'm pretty sure the overgrowth had something to do with witchcraft and our powers being one with nature, but I'd yet to have that conversation with Leo, Ted, or my mother. As a matter of fact, there was still a lot of ground to cover when it came to this secret life of mine.

"Liam, what are you doing here? Is everything okay?"

"Yes, everything's fine. I just came to tell you that Flo is being moved to a prison in New Haven until her trial." Liam tilted his head as he breathed in deeply, and that attractive smirk pulled at his lips. I really needed to drop this insane interest I had in him. It wouldn't be wise to get involved with an officer of the law when I couldn't even come close to explaining my family. "Is that coffee I smell?"

"Don't pretend for one second that you don't know my secret," I said, wagging my finger as I took a step back and allowed him to enter. Heidi's ponytail seemed to be swaying back and forth as her entire body practically screamed *go for it*. She didn't know the truth, either, and that was very depressing. "Come on in. Heidi and I were just getting ready to head into town. She's got to get back to the city to give Patrick his car, and I need to open up the shop after brunch."

Seeing as it was Sunday, the tea shop was only open from eleven o'clock to four o'clock. I liked these days, because it allowed me to continue my search for the elusive spell book. The reason my mother was coming back to town on Wednesday was because she'd come up with something called a locator spell.

I really hoped it worked, because my learning had all come

to a complete halt…with the exception of what little I could find over the Internet. I was astounded by what could be found with a bit of motivation and digging in the right areas.

Leo was constantly telling me I needed to be careful not to alert anyone to my newfound powers, but that was the nice thing about computers—I was hidden behind a screen of anonymity.

"I have a meeting with Detective Swanson, which is why I'm here or else I would have waited for you to come into town." Liam stepped inside, his dark eyes only giving away a glimpse of surprise when he surveyed the interior of the cottage. "Did you do this in the weeks you've been here? I'm not sure how you had the time to decorate between learning to be a businesswoman and solving a murder."

"I'd love to take the credit, but this was Nan all the way. She always was a bit eccentric."

*Eccentric? She used black magic on me. I'm a Persian leopard in a munchkin cat's body. She bypassed eccentric about a million years ago.*

A quick glance confirmed that Leo was hanging over the ledge of the loft between two of the spindles.

"I offered to move in to keep Raven company, but she's being selfish and won't make me a partner in the tea shop," Heidi complained, though her broad smile told Liam that she was joking. She couldn't see Leo from where she was, and that was probably a good thing. She might very well try to go up the stairs and corral him. "You could always make her a deputy while I take over the store. It can't be too hard to work those handcuff thingies."

*I might be in love. She is quick with those comebacks, isn't she?*

I couldn't stop my cheeks from flushing at what Heidi was implicating, so I quickly changed the topic of conversation.

There was no reason to give Leo more ammunition, either.

"You mentioned something about Flo being moved to a prison in New Haven?"

"Yes, and it looks like you won't need to testify. She confessed."

Liam's gaze had finally settled on me, but not before I saw his interest in the various carvings in the coffee table. I didn't want him to ask questions about the markings, so I moved a bit until I could rest my hand on the back of the stool Heidi had vacated to pet Leo. From her expression, my movements weren't natural in the least.

"That's great news, but I don't understand."

"Flo has pleaded guilty by reason of insanity. There will be a competency hearing, of course. Whether she spends her time in a prison or a mental institution is another thing altogether." Liam held up the newspaper that had been in his hand. "The *Paramour Bay Times* has the article, and I thought you'd like to read it."

*You're not buying this, are you? The good ole sheriff wants to do more than—*

"Thank you." I unfolded the thin newspaper, surprised to find a picture of Flo in an orange jumpsuit being escorted to a police van. She didn't look any better in orange than I did. "Is it sad that a part of me feels bad for her?"

*The old bat tried to kill us!*

"Let's face it," Liam responded with a commiserating shake of his head, "Flo is not altogether there mentally. I can't believe none of us picked up on her breakdown. I mean, killing a man because she thought he was going to steal tea leaves she believed made her look younger? You're just lucky she didn't try to come after you."

"Here, let me see," Heidi exclaimed, leaning over the island to hold out her hand. "I never went into the diner, so I don't know what Flo looks like."

"Take a look. That's what jail does to a person." Liam pointed toward the newspaper Heidi was now looking at to satisfy her curiosity. "Flo has definitely aged in the week and a half she's been in prison."

I shifted back and forth on the knee-high boots I was wearing underneath my long skirt. This was one of those times where I experienced the stabbing of guilt over keeping secrets from those I cared about, as well as the residents of Paramour Bay. They had no idea that Nan had been a witch all these years or that my mother and I had followed in her footsteps to varying degrees.

It wasn't fair.

I was technically all alone.

*You've got me.*

The sincere sentiment caught me by surprise, and apparently had done so to Leo. Another glance up toward the loft revealed Leo licking his paw, as if his words meant nothing. In reality, they meant everything.

*I love you, too, Leo.*

It was a good thing Liam and Heidi hadn't known Leo was there, because he'd vanished right before my eyes. And that was okay.

My new life encompassed a talking cat, my own Lurch who goes by the name of Ted, a town full of quirky residents, and a handsome sheriff. Not to mention that my best friend was able to visit me at least every other weekend, and my mother was willing to extend her hand into a life she'd left behind years ago.

And let's not forget witchcraft.

I was a witch.

A real witch.

And there was no other place I'd rather be than right here in Paramour Bay.

~ THE END ~

Thank you so much for reading Magical Blend! Don't miss out on more exciting shenanigans that take place in Paramour Bay as the series continues with Bewitching Blend.

kennedylayne.com/bewitching-blend.html

*Welcome back to Paramour Bay as USA Today Bestselling Author Kennedy Layne continues her cozy paranormal mystery series that will have you brewing up a cup of tea well past midnight...*

It's been two months since Raven Marigold discovered she was a witch, and she is handling her situation with grace. Well, if you discount the fact that she caught her blouse on fire or made her cat's tail go numb for four hours. The bottom line is that Raven is succeeding in her pursuit of this new mystical life she's been given.

Someone must have missed that memo, though. Raven finds herself smack dab in the middle of another murder investigation. Every piece of evidence points to the town treasurer as being the guilty party, but she isn't so sure the case is that cut and dried.

It is then that Raven gets the brilliant idea of using a bit of witchcraft to help out the handsome, young sheriff. After all, what could go wrong with a bewitching blend, an enchanted spell book, and a haunted inn on the edge of town?

# Books by Kennedy Layne

## Paramour Bay Mysteries
Magical Blend
Bewitching Blend

## Office Roulette Series
Means (Office Roulette, Book One)
Motive (Office Roulette, Book Two)
Opportunity (Office Roulette, Book Three)

## Keys to Love Series
Unlocking Fear (Keys to Love, Book One)
Unlocking Secrets (Keys to Love, Book Two)
Unlocking Lies (Keys to Love, Book Three)
Unlocking Shadows (Keys to Love, Book Four)
Unlocking Darkness (Keys to Love, Book Five)

## Surviving Ashes Series
Essential Beginnings (Surviving Ashes, Book One)
Hidden Ashes (Surviving Ashes, Book Two)
Buried Flames (Surviving Ashes, Book Three)
Endless Flames (Surviving Ashes, Book Four)
Rising Flames (Surviving Ashes, Book Five)

## CSA Case Files Series
Captured Innocence (CSA Case Files 1)
Sinful Resurrection (CSA Case Files 2)
Renewed Faith (CSA Case Files 3)

# ABOUT THE AUTHOR

First and foremost, I love life. I love that I'm a wife, mother, daughter, sister… and a writer.

I am one of the lucky women in this world who gets to do what makes them happy. As long as I have a cup of coffee (maybe two or three) and my laptop, the stories evolve themselves and I try to do them justice. I draw my inspiration from a retired Marine Master Sergeant that swept me off of my feet and has drawn me into a world that fulfills all of my deepest and darkest desires. Erotic romance, military men, intrigue, with a little bit of kinky chili pepper (his recipe), fill my head and there is nothing more satisfying than making the hero and heroine fulfill their destinies.

Thank you for having joined me on their journeys…

Email: kennedylayneauthor@gmail.com

Facebook: facebook.com/kennedy.layne.94

Twitter: twitter.com/KennedyL_Author

Website: www.kennedylayne.com

Newsletter: www.kennedylayne.com/newslettertext.html

Made in the USA
San Bernardino, CA
14 October 2018